ROSE
IN A
STORM

ROSE
IN A
STORM

A NOVEL

JON
KATZ

VILLARD ⓥ NEW YORK

Copyright © 2010 by Jon Katz

Published in the United States by Villard Books, an imprint of The Random House Publishing Group, a division of Random House, Inc., New York.

VILLARD BOOKS and VILLARD & "V" CIRCLED Design are registered trademarks of Random House, Inc.

ISBN 978-0-345-50265-0
eBook ISBN 978-0-345-52296-2

Printed in the United States of America on acid-free paper

www.villard.com

First Edition

Photograph on page vii by Jon Katz

Book design by Susan Turner

TO THE REAL
ROSE

There is no greater glory than to die for love.

—GABRIEL GARCÍA MÁRQUEZ,
Love in the Time of Cholera

ROSE
IN A
STORM

ONE

Inside the farmhouse Rose lifted her head and pricked up her ears. She heard the troubled wheezing of a ewe. From the window, through the dark, she could see mist, mud, and the reddish shadows of the barns. She pictured the herd of sheep lying still, spread out behind the feeder.

Raising her nose toward the pasture, she smelled the rich, sticky scent of birth, of lamb. She smelled manure and fear.

She heard a gasp, the sound of death or desperation, and then one ewe calling to the others in alarm. She stood and padded quickly from the window to the side of the farmer's bed, then looked up at his sleeping face. She barked once, insistently and loudly.

Sam, the farmer, startled awake from a dream of Katie in the dark January night. He muttered, "Are you sure?" and mumbled something about a night's sleep, but got out of bed, pulling on pants and a shirt.

He knew better than to ignore Rose, especially at lambing

time. She seemed to have a sort of map of the farm inside her head, a picture of how things ought to be. Whenever something was wrong or out of place—an animal sick, a fence down, an unwelcome intruder—she knew it instantly, and called attention to it, sniffing, barking, circling. She constantly updated the map, it seemed to Sam.

Occasionally her map failed or confused her—but that was rare. Sam saw to it that Rose was always with him, that she was apprised of everything that came and went—every animal, every machine—so she could keep her mental inventory.

Among his friends, Sam called Rose his farm manager. They had been together for six years, ever since he had driven over to the Clark farm in Easton and seen a litter of border collie/shepherd mix pups. He had still been debating with himself about whether to get a herding dog—he had no idea how to train one, and no time to do it, anyway.

But, perhaps picking up the scent of sheep, Rose ran right over to him, looking so eager to get to work, even at eight weeks old, that he brought her home. A few weeks after she arrived, some sheep had wandered through an unlatched gate and across the road, and Rose shot out of the house through the newly installed dog door, corralled them, and marched them back, working on instinct alone. She certainly had no help from Sam, who wasn't even aware that the sheep were at liberty. The two had been working side by side ever since.

From then on, Sam would shake his head whenever he saw the elaborate, highly choreographed herding trials on television. Rose grew into the role on her own; she simply seemed to know what to do. The farm, he told his friends, was the world's greatest trainer. And the sheep did what she told them to, which was all Sam really cared about. Get them from one place to another. Didn't have to be pretty, though sometimes it was beautiful.

The relationship had grown way beyond anything Sam understood at first, or even imagined. It was more like a partnership, he had told Katie, an understanding subtler than words. It was something he lived, not something he thought much about.

I think you love that dog more than me, Katie would sometimes joke. Sam would blush and stammer. She's just a dog, he would say, because he could not say what Rose truly meant to him.

Now he could tell from the urgency of Rose's bark that something was wrong. She kept tilting her ears to the pasture, agitated, eager to get outside.

So on this cold and windswept night, Sam, a tall, thin man with what had once been a ready smile and a full head of reddish-brown hair, went downstairs and got a flashlight, pulled on a jacket and boots, and he and Rose walked out the back door and into the night. Even in the dark, in the reflected light of the moon, he could see the glow of her fiercely bright-blue eyes.

THE FARMHOUSE SAT at the bottom of a gentle, rolling pasture. By the back door, there were two paths. The one to the left led out into the woods, and the one to the right ran toward the two barns and the pasture gates.

The first barn was big, filled with hay up in the loft and tractors, and sometimes cows, down below. A shed was attached to the big barn, which housed equipment and supplies, as well as some feed. Farther up the hill was a large pole barn.

A three-sided structure with the fourth side open to the air, it allowed the sheep to be outside, which they preferred, while still offering some shelter from the elements. When they were kept inside a closed barn, they got fearful, claustrophobic, bleated day and night. Anyway, it was the way Sam's father had done it. The three buildings formed a triangle: the farmhouse at the bottom, the big barn off to one side nearby, the pole barn a hundred yards up the hill. The cows were in the other pasture on the far side of the barn.

A few hundred feet from the farmhouse, the path led to a gate that connected to a fence encircling all of the pastures and barns. Sam was proud of that fence. He'd spent years shoring and patching it, and in the past year or so, no animal had slipped out, or in.

As they neared the barn, Sam finally saw in the beam of light from his flashlight what Rose had heard and sensed, up behind the building. He moved faster, opening the pasture gate. Rose raced through and ran to the struggling ewe. Sam retrieved his sack of medical equipment from the barn and hurried behind the dog up a path well worn by the animals, marked by manure and ice-encrusted mud, pungent even in winter. The big barn was on the right, looming like a great battleship, its lights sending small beams out into the dark, foggy pasture. That old barn had a lot of stories to tell.

The lambing shed where Sam had put this pregnant ewe a few days earlier was also open on one side, though protected from the snow and wind. An open hatchway led from the lambing shed inside the barn to an area warmed by heat lamps and lined with hay and straw, where the ewes could take their newborn lambs. With this arrangement, they were outside when they went into labor, so they could be near the other sheep, and Sam could still see and hear them from the house. Or at least Rose could.

He trained his light on the sick ewe, number 89. Her wheezing had calmed, which was an ominous sign, and she lay still, on her side, in the corner of the pen in a bed of hay.

Rose waited for Sam to open the birthing pen gate, then rushed in to the mother and attempted to rouse her, nipping at her nose and chest.

Sam opened his bag and pulled out scissors, forceps, bandages, syringes, a jar of iodine, antibiotics, and some rope and salve. He was serious and calm as he followed Rose's lead, this small black and white dog, with those piercing eyes, moving with speed and confidence.

THE OTHER SHEEP gathered in the pole barn up the hill, watching, intent and anxious. Rose glanced up at the crowd of ewes, and at the Blackface, their leader, who had appeared at the front of the flock. Rose's eyes and posture gave clear instructions—stay back, stay away from Sam—and they obeyed.

If necessary, she would use her teeth, pulling some wool to get things moving, or to stop things from moving. She rarely needed to do that. But tonight, particularly since there was no food around the lambing area, Rose knew they would keep their distance. The sheep wanted no part of a human or a dog in the middle of the night.

It was black and cold, and the ground was icy. Rose saw and smelled the amniotic fluid puddling under the ewe. Rose could see the almost imperceptible movement of the ewe's stomach, hear the faint breath, see the moisture in her eyes, the stream from her nostrils. She could hear the faintest of heartbeats.

She could smell the ewe's struggle.

Rose and Sam had done this before, many times.

Having failed to get the ewe to her feet, Rose backed up while Sam set up his light, kneeled down, rolled up his sleeves. She watched him rub salve on his hands before turning the ewe and plunging his arm into the dying mother, finding the lamb stuck in the uterine canal.

The smell was intense, and troubling. This was a bad sign. Lambs didn't last very long after the water had broken.

Sam muttered and cursed. He turned the lamb's feet until they were pointed in the right direction, then he grunted, pulled, and pulled again. Finally, Rose saw him draw out his hand, and with it, the lamb. The small, matted creature was not moving.

Sam dipped his pocketknife in a bottle and then used it to cut the umbilical cord. Then he stood, lifted the lamb by its feet, and swung it, left and right, in the cold air, to get its heart beating. The lamb was slick with fluids, and the air was frigid. Lambs can die quickly in these conditions. If they're healthy, their mothers will usually guide them through the hatchway to the warmth of the heat lamps.

Rose barked, excited. The lamb suddenly coughed and wheezed. It was alive. Rose ran around to the ewe's face and began nipping at her nose, urging her to her feet.

The dog and the farmer worked with urgency. The cold was biting and Rose felt the sting of it in her paws. Her whiskers were covered in ice. She needed to get the ewe up quickly, had to get her to clean her lamb. And the lamb needed nourishment.

* * *

SAM PULLED OUT a plastic bottle with sheep's milk that he had stored in the freezer and thawed, putting it gently in the lamb's mouth. He pulled a syringe from his other pocket—a vitamin booster, for strength and energy—and gave the lamb a shot. Rose kept working to get the mother up, so she and her lamb could bond by smell and know each other.

The ewe began to stir, looking at Rose. The dog did not waver or back off, but barked and lunged, nipped and kept her eyes locked on the ewe's.

The ewe closed her eyes, reopened them. She was suddenly alarmed, breathing more heavily now, as she struggled to get to her feet. Afterbirth trailed from under her tail.

Sam carefully put the lamb down and came over to help, pulling the ewe up gently. She was disoriented, panicky, and as soon as she was upright she tried to bolt. Rose headed her off. She and Sam knew all too well that when ewes ran, they could forget the smell of their lambs and abandon them entirely. That was not going to happen, had *never* happened when Rose was there.

Rose held the ewe to the spot while Sam positioned the lamb beside her. Then he ran into the barn and came back with some water laced with molasses syrup for the ewe. She lapped it up greedily while the lamb searched for its mother's nipple. The ewe seemed to gain strength, returning to the world, becoming aware of her baby.

The ewe began to call out to her lamb. Now protective, she turned, lowered her head at Rose, and charged, butting her, and catching her off guard.

"Head's up, Rose!" said Sam.

Rose was sometimes unprepared for how powerful the mothering instinct was in ewes once it kicked in and they bonded with their babies. It was a testing time for her, as the formerly compliant ewes changed, and she was suddenly, sometimes violently, challenged. She always regained control, with her body, her eyes, her teeth, and her ferocious determination, which eventually wore down even the most maternal ewe, even though it sometimes left Rose bruised or limping. After a time, they became sheep again, doing what they were supposed to do.

The vet once told Sam that Rose weighed thirty-seven pounds, and that any one of those two- and three-hundred-pound ewes or rams could have stomped or butted her senseless, but they didn't know they could. Rose had to make sure they never knew.

SAM LOOKED UP and saw that it had begun snowing lightly, and the wind was picking up. He was huffing hard on his hands, looking up at the sky. Rose looked up, too, and felt a stirring in all of her senses.

Sam appeared different to Rose than he used to, quieter, not as strong, not as clear-headed. A lot of things were different since the night Katie had been taken from the house.

The very map of the farm had changed.

She watched Sam as he worked silently, purposefully, toweling off the lamb. Once he was sure the mother had the smell of the lamb, he picked it up in a cloth sling. It was time to get it under the heat lamps and onto a pile of straw. There the mother would finish cleaning her baby, and the baby would find her teats and drink some more, getting warm and dry, and the ewe could bond with him—it was a ram—and know his cry. The two would nestle up together and talk to each other in a language all their own.

Sam was now backing up to the hatchway, and the ewe looked around frantically. Rose kept her distance, a bit away and behind her, so that she wouldn't panic and head for the other sheep, who were still watching from the pole barn.

The ewe darted a few feet up the hill. Rose dashed ahead of her and brought her back. They repeated this two or three times, Rose and the ewe, in a kind of a dance, Rose anticipating where the ewe would go and blocking that route. Even though her lamb was being carried in that direction, it was unnatural for the ewe to move away from her flock, and toward the barn, especially with a human and a dog. Only the ewe's intensifying mothering instincts kept her from running off. That and Rose in her face, whenever she looked or turned to go up the hill.

Finally at the hatchway entrance to the barn, the ewe froze. Rose watched her look up the hill, then toward her lamb. Rose saw that she was still thinking of bolting up to the pole barn, to the Blackface, to the safety and comfort of the other sheep.

Sam backed into the barn, making sure the ewe could see him and the lamb in his arms. He opened the lambing pen gate, then turned on the heat lamps and put the baby down in the warming glow. The lamb bleated, and the ewe bleated in response, rushing through the hatchway and into the pen.

Rose kept the mother in until she settled down there. The ewe eventually forgot Rose, and nosed the lamb under the lamp and onto the hay. She began licking him. Sam closed and tied the plastic fencing of the makeshift pen. The ewe, exhausted, would let her baby feed, and then the two of them would sleep.

Sam turned away to check the wiring of the heat lamp and bring some fresh hay. Rose sat down, calming also. Her job was done. But in less than a minute she stood again and turned away, limping slightly from the butting of her shoulder.

"Okay, girl," Sam said to Rose as he shone the flashlight around to see if the other pregnant ewes were up to anything. Rose did not understand his words but understood the tone of voice, his approval. And she also understood it as the end of this work.

Rose smelled the warm, rich mother's milk, heard the sound of suckling. The timeless map, a compilation of countless memories and experiences and images, was as it should be, and now updated to include one new creature.

Sam slid the door shut.

Rose followed him to the gate and then trotted toward the house. Sam walked on ahead of her, but on the stoop, she paused for a moment. Something made her look up again at the predawn slate sky.

Rose felt the storm coming, smelled snow and heavy air. She remembered other storms, the snow and wind and killing cold. She felt a flash of deep alarm run through her like a bolt of lightning. The hair on her back and neck came up. Sam called for her, but she waited a moment longer before following him inside.

TWO

S AM PADDED UPSTAIRS TO BED AND FELL SLEEP ALMOST instantly. Rose drifted to the back of the second floor, into a spare room used for storage where she often curled up on a bed of old towels and rags, sometimes taking a bone or stick with her, though usually not.

Sam rarely went into that room; it was Rose's secret resting chamber, a place of dreams. Perhaps the only place she was calm, away from work. Sometime before dawn, when the farm was quiet and Sam was off in a deep sleep, as he was now, she allowed herself to sleep, too, hidden away.

At Winston the rooster's first crowing, Rose got up, ready and alert by the time Sam awakened soon after and came downstairs. She took a few pieces of kibble that he poured for her, but she was too distracted for food.

The morning was gray, ominous. The snow was falling lightly, unconvincing, but Rose knew it would be heavier soon.

She moved quickly through the living room to the back

door of the farmhouse, where she looked down at Sam's feet, and saw that he was wearing his old boots. She whined a bit in excitement—those shoes meant they would soon be working together.

Rose ran out the back door, along the pasture fence and up to the gate. Sam walked behind her, as briskly as he could. She moved in circles around him—always in motion, looking left and right, listening. When she was working, her body was focused, buzzing; all of her instincts, senses, and energy raced at their most intense.

Rose waited at the gate for Sam, her head lowered, her right paw raised, poised to proceed. She looked up at the leader of the sheep—the Blackface with the brown eyes who had a dignity and bearing different from the rest of the flock.

The Blackface froze, and so did the other sheep. Rose held them there to keep them away from Sam while he got their grain. The sheep sometimes charged down the hill, running into Sam, even knocking him down if Rose wasn't there, head lowered, her eyes fixing them in place. If any sheep moved an inch, she would charge up the hill, get close to their faces and force them to back up. She held them there until the farmer said, "Okay, girl," and then she would rush up behind them and drive them down to the feeder. Sam would be gone by then, safely in the barn.

Rose had been born with an understanding that, where sheep were involved, she should never waiver. If the sheep ever sensed that she wasn't sure, things would quickly fall apart.

Rose sat by the feeder for the next hour, watching the sheep eat. Sam had gone back into the farmhouse. When a car pulled up, Rose barked, and Sam reappeared at the door. A woman whose perfume caught Rose's attention from some distance got out of the car and took a long and appraising look around the farm. Rose loped up to challenge her, but the woman greeted her by softly murmuring her name. She did not reach out to pet her. Rose was taken with her boots, which smelled of animal waste. In her mind, Rose saw a horse.

Sam approached the solidly built woman, who stood waiting in the driveway beside the big barn, and welcomed her with a hug. He began to make a series of noises, as humans often did, gesturing to this woman, who seemed uncomfortable in the gathering wind. He looked her directly in the eye, as was his way when talking to people, but she looked away.

"Sam, I know this has been an awful year for you, what with losing Katie and all. We'll get the best price we can."

Sam shifted his feet, zipped up his work sweatshirt, and looked up through the light snowflakes at the gray sky. He and Katie had been thinking of converting the business of Granville Farm, located in a valley of the southern Adirondacks, and starting to grow and sell organic produce. The old-school farmers were going under, one by one, but organic farms were surviving. Sam and Katie were excited about the prospect of change. Katie had sent for the Cornell University catalogue and was thinking of taking some online courses on the new agricultural economy.

Sam bred and sold sheep and beef cows, sending meat to New York City restaurants with other farmers. He also rotated his crops—alfalfa, potatoes, corn, among others.

Now, though, with Katie's death two months earlier, everything had changed.

He didn't have the kind of energy he used to. He no longer thought he had the heart to start over, even though everyone told him to take his time, to wait before making any decisions.

Sam turned back to the woman. "I appreciate it, Ginny. I'll call you. Meantime, Agway Farmer's Service says we're set to get a real big one down from Canada. I just hope the power doesn't go out right away."

ROSE STOOD by Sam's side, watching the sky, then the sheep, paying no attention to the sounds coming out of the two people until she heard the word "Katie."

Rose knew that Katie was not in the farmhouse, but she did not know where she had gone. Rose watched for Katie every day, but she was not in reach of her sight or her hearing. She did, however, smell her—her smell was everywhere in the house, on the floors, in the closets and bed, in the kitchen, on doorknobs and cabinet handles. But Rose couldn't place Katie on the map. Still, she was there.

Sam talked less now—he moved slowly, worked less, routinely sat alone on his sofa in the big room in front of the woodstove. Rose often came to lie near him, but he did not touch her, nor would she have accepted that. She insisted on a certain space between her and all living things, except when she was battling sheep.

But she was conscious of Sam's great sadness. Sitting with Sam next to the woodstove also became part of her work. In this new routine, being with him had become another task.

SAM AND THE WOMAN outside were still talking to each other. Rose was now paying attention to the tone, to Sam's tenseness and anticipation. She also felt a shifting in her consciousness— an arousal. She was coming to know something, to feel it: This would be a massive, disturbing storm. Her body was alive with the sense of it approaching.

She felt danger in her body, saw it in her mind. And she called up her own kind of memory, the images of many lives in many places that she carried in her head, heart, and bones.

She saw mountains of snow, felt bitter cold, the humbling power of the winter wind moving across open fields.

She recalled the experience of clawing through snow, crawling over and under it. Of food buried in ice, paths blocked by drifts, pasture after pasture covered in white. Of animals struggling, starving.

Images whirred and rushed and hissed and blew through her mind. Like a wheel in a carnival, they slowed and stopped.

THE WOMAN got in her car and drove away. Rose and Sam looked up at the sky.

"I would hate to leave this place, girl," he said. "Let's go to work."

She rose to her feet, alert.

"We're going to put some hay up in the pole barn, and put out feed for the donkey, cows, and chickens. Best we can do. Then we'll see what we see."

Sam often spoke this way—in his work voice—laying out the chores ahead, and in this way he'd taught Rose many words. Mostly they related to Katie, sheep, work, or the farm.

Sam saw dogs as many farmers did. He didn't believe in coddling or praising them. They were animals, and they had a job to do, as did he, and they both were expected to do it. He didn't believe in treats, and hated the chirpy "up" voices some people used to talk to and reward dogs, voices that usually made Rose flatten her ears and move away. Rose loved work, and in his mind that was reward enough. He respected her, as he believed she respected him, and praise was not necessary. Approval was different.

Dogs were not children. They came and went, took care of themselves, slept inside at night if they wanted to. They had their own lives.

Just then Rose looked up at the sheep on the hill. She saw something else that made her stop, freeze, growl. She moved forward, her eyes trained on the hill, at the upper pasture. Sam turned and tried to follow her gaze.

"What is it—" Then he stopped. He saw it, too. Something was up in the right far corner of the pasture, by the gate. Rose, uttering a low growl, began moving up toward the lower gate. Sam followed and the two of them made their way up the hill.

About a third of the way up, he saw what Rose had noticed minutes earlier. A small doe was caught in the pasture gate, wedged between the metal end of it and the wooden fencepost, where the gate was latched by a thick chain.

The doe had tried to squeeze through the opening, probably during the night—sensing the coming storm and foraging for food—and gotten stuck. Her head was facing them, and she was twisting piteously, her eyes darting wildly.

Rose walked up ahead of Sam, slowly, as she always moved in the presence of wild animals. Sam did not call her back, or keep her away. Rose was not a dog to charge a deer or skunk or raccoon. She avoided them if possible, and, if not, circled them warily.

As Sam got farther up the hill, he saw that blood was seeping from a cut on the doe's nose. She was little bigger than a fawn, and her sides were rubbed raw from trying to push through the gate. The space would tighten when she surged forward. Sam winced. It must have been painful.

He approached carefully. The doe began bleating, thrashing her limbs toward Sam and Rose, whose approach deepened her panic. Sam knew how dangerous wounded or trapped deer could be, as they slashed out with their sharp hooves. He thought about going to get his rifle and shooting the doe to put her out of her misery. He had to get the farm ready for the storm, and he couldn't afford to hurt himself or endanger Rose. But he kept moving up toward her instead. Looking into her wide brown eyes, he saw the fear in them.

He was not a hunter, couldn't understand the idea of trapping an animal, or lying in wait for it in the woods and shooting it. It didn't bother him that others did it, it just wasn't something he could see himself doing.

Sam realized that if he could get close enough to reach over the doe, he could lift the chain up and the gate might swing forward and release. Her wounds were serious, and he knew he couldn't leave her there. He either had to free her or shoot her.

As he approached, the doe kicked her legs forward, crying out in a piercing, surprisingly loud voice. She slashed her front hooves in a scissor kick, catching and tearing the sleeve of his coat.

Sam jumped back. He moved closer, and the doe bleated and kicked out again. He reached forward a dozen times, but there was simply no way to get close enough. He pulled a stick off a maple tree, attempting to reach and unlock the gate with it, but she lashed out at the stick with her hooves and broke it.

All this time, Rose was behind him, edging closer, watching. Sam waited to see if the doe would grow comfortable with him, or else grow too tired to fight. He tried talking to the deer, soothing her, throwing some twigs with dead leaves down to distract her.

After a while, he decided to switch his approach. He told Rose to stay, then started down the hill to the barn. Rose moved a few feet down the slope, lay down in a crouch, and watched the doe, who fell silent, staring right back. She had finally stopped struggling.

Sam returned with an armful of hay, and also an old Winchester .30-06 rifle. He threw the hay on the ground and leaned the rifle against the fence.

The doe wouldn't sniff or eat the hay.

"Come on, girl," he pleaded. "I'm not going to hurt you. Give me a chance to get you out of this. I'm running out of time." Sometimes, Sam knew, animals responded to tone of voice. If you were calm, they might be, too.

The ground was stained with blood.

He looked over at the rifle.

Suddenly, he was aware of Rose moving up behind him on his left. He and Rose had been in a hundred scrapes together, from aggressive geese to rampaging rams, runaway cows, encroaching foxes, rabid raccoons, and nasty feral cats. She always came up with a plan.

"What have you got here, Rose?" he asked, as if she could answer. Rose didn't look at Sam. She was too focused on the doe.

Sam watched as Rose moved out and away from the doe, growling and, occasionally, barking. He couldn't fathom what she was doing, but then he saw the doe's head turn slowly to the right, and away from him. Rose edged forward, bit by bit, and as the deer slashed out at her with her hooves, bleating, Rose kept barking, moving from side to side, in and out, but staying just out of reach.

The doe had forgotten about Sam, her eyes locked onto Rose, who kept moving and making noise. Sam saw an opportunity and edged forward, holding the butt of the rifle out to ward off any kicks. The doe never took her eyes off Rose as Sam, holding the rifle out, reached forward with his right hand, and pulled the chain up off of the latch. The gate swung forward, releasing the doe.

Rose backed quickly away, and so did Sam. The deer, startled, froze. Then in an instant she turned and disappeared into the winter brush.

Rose and Sam stood there, at the top of the hill, looking at the blood and fur left on the pole and gate.

"Hope she makes it," Sam said, quietly. He closed the gate and refastened the chain.

Silently, the two of them walked back down the hill.

WHEN THEY GOT to the bottom, Sam went into the farmhouse to stash the gun but keep it handy, and Rose felt another rush of blood, up and down her spine, and a sharpening of her senses. She looked over toward the pasture, to where Brownie, the gargantuan Swiss steer, was staring at her with his enormous brown eyes. He was monstrous; he towered over her, and even over Sam, standing well above the other cows and steers. He was waiting.

Rose was easy around Brownie, and associated the name with him, as Sam often spoke it around him. She knew by now that he, like the other cows and steers, was ultimately doomed: He would either die or leave. For her, it was one of life's clearest lessons.

She also knew how to get him to move when he didn't want to budge but Sam needed him to. If Rose came by quickly, nipped two or three times at a spot on his legs just below his knees, and then darted away even quicker, Brownie would be startled into moving. The little dog was masterly at annoying Brownie without actually putting him into a panic, especially since he could have crushed her if he turned aggressive.

The cows and steers had felt the storm coming earlier in the morning. All the animals were slowing, withdrawing into themselves, preparing and conserving their energy.

Sam emerged from the farmhouse and opened the pasture gate. The sheep always tried to get into the barn at feeding time, because they knew the grain was there. Rose did not permit it. She stood in the door and looked at them fiercely. The bravest of them inched down the pasture, but didn't come closer.

One wether took a belligerent step toward Rose, his head down, daring her to stop him. She marched up the slope, moving directly into his face, then darted to grab a mouthful of wool, pulling it right off his head. He lowered his face again, and she nipped him on the nose. Startled, he backed away, giving up.

Once in a while one of them would rebel, take a chance, overwhelmed by the instinct to eat. But they never got past Rose.

As Sam walked into the barn, the two cats, Eve and Jane, appeared, as they always did, out of the rafters. Rose often saw them catch mice and toy with them before they killed them. Cats were murderous one moment, flirtatious the next, unfathomable to her, deceitful, slippery. All the work they did was in killing, dismembering prey and then playing with the parts before scattering them around. Rose grasped the notion of hunting well enough, but the savage side of these cats was beyond her ken. Their territory—the vast hay-bale mountains in the barn—was the one district on the farm Rose avoided. It was a place of bats, mice, and barn swallows—a lot of fluttering and skittering—not the realm of a dog.

Sam checked the chicken feed and pulled a sack down from the shelf. He filled the feeder high, as he always did before a storm, and checked the heated water tub that the cats and chickens used.

He climbed up the ladder to the platform he'd built for the chicken roosts, to keep them up off the floor and safe from predators—the occasional badger or raccoon or fox that might wander into the barn. The hens could hop up onto the platform and climb into their roosts, and it was still wide enough to store some hay and feed.

There was an upper barn window just above the roosts, which Sam kept closed to keep animals out.

Eve and Jane paraded along the wooden rails. Rose ignored them, since they were not subject to her supervision or authority. They were not interested in her, either.

Through the window she saw Brownie, who appeared curious, looking into the barn. Sometimes he got some grain, if Sam had time or it was especially cold. Grain gave the animals energy. Otherwise just hay.

No grain this morning. Sam was moving too quickly, getting ready.

Winston, the farm's ancient rooster, hobbled over to see if Sam would drop any seed on the ground. Winston rarely left the barn these days—his legs were too unsteady—but he made plenty of noise just the same. Rose treated him with respect. He was the oldest animal on the farm and had seen a lot.

* * *

By MID-MORNING the light snow that had begun the night before had petered out. Sam knew it would start back up with a vengeance soon. But for now it was a beautiful day. The slate-gray sky was set off by the bright-red barn. It was windy and cold and he moved around the farm with an increasing sense of urgency as he prepared for the storm. He'd not yet eaten anything that day, but he did not stop working.

A sense of alertness had swept the farm and its creatures, a stillness, a formality perhaps. The word was passed about the storm in the way animals exchange an understanding, something that Sam had seen many times before. The animals bunched together, raised their noses and ears to the sky. Their eyes were open, vigilant. The feeling had spread to the steers and cows, to the chickens and the sheep, to Carol the donkey, to the barn cats. It even spread to the three goats—troublesome, greedy creatures, who found cause to defy Rose at every turn.

Sam climbed the stairs up to the hayloft.

He piled up some bales by the back door of the barn and slid it open. He fired up the tractor, attached it to the hay wagon, hefted another twenty bales on, and pulled it up to the pole barn.

Sam came back down the hill and filled the water tanks. There was no point, he knew, in putting out too much extra grain, as the animals would eat it all immediately, get bloated and sick, but he put out more than usual to give them some extra energy and strength. He tossed a basket of corn kernels out for the chickens. He took a bag of dry cat kibble, slit it open partway, then heaved it up on a shelf in the barn. All of this would give the animals an extra day or two if they were stranded or if the feeders were buried in snow.

The cats, sensing something unusual, climbed up to the top of the bales to watch. Sam saw that Rose followed them with her eyes.

Outside the barn door, Carol the donkey brayed, and the sheep had gathered, hoping for grain, anxious to eat. Rose glared at them, backing them up the hill. Carol eyed Rose carefully. A couple of years earlier she had kicked Rose without warning, nearly killing her.

Carol had been treated poorly and neglected for years before the farm she used to live on went under and Sam took her in. She had no real purpose on Sam's farm, although he liked to claim she was a guard animal. It was true that she was protective of the flock, always taking the sheep's side. And she wouldn't hesitate to charge a coyote or stray dog if it came near.

While Sam checked the deicers on the water tanks, which would go out if the power went, Rose lay down and studied the sheep, looking them over one by one, challenging the difficult ones, giving them plenty of eye.

Sam got back into the tractor and hauled straw up to the pole barn and spread it around to make warm bedding for the sheep, then he stuffed the wooden feeders. As he drove, Rose ran alongside the tractor, barking at it, trying to herd it, perhaps, or move it to a different spot. Sam yelled at her to get away, but these were commands she ignored, or perhaps simply didn't hear. Sam was never sure, though he had his suspicions.

Because there wasn't enough room to drive the tractor up to the goat pen, which was up a slope and beyond a narrow gate, Sam had to carry hay there by hand. He made a half dozen trips to stow bales under a flimsy plywood roof. He suspected the snow would cover them up quickly—the roof was designed as protection from rain, not blowing snow, but it might keep enough snow off that the goats might have half a chance to dig the food out.

Rose watched but kept her distance. She had as little use for goats as she did for barn cats, and they were almost completely incorrigible, ignoring her, or even taunting her, if she tried to move them. The goats were potentially functional, part of Sam's experimentation with organic milk and cheese. Still, he disliked them almost as much as Rose did, as they were loud, obnoxious, and nearly impossible to control. They were a world apart from his beef cows, who loved nothing more than to graze quietly, off by themselves.

Sam had also sold spinach and carrots to farmers' markets in New York and Philadelphia. He used to talk to Rose while they worked, outlining the business plans he and Katie were developing. Farming needed to grow food to survive, in addition to raising dairy cows. He said farmers had to change, and that he intended for Granville Farm to try different things. He knew, of course, that Rose didn't understand what he was saying, but she clearly liked being consulted, having Sam's attention, and she cocked her head intently as if she were getting every word.

Since Katie's death, though, Sam rarely spoke to Rose about his business plans, or much else.

He rarely spoke at all.

Sam put the plow attachment on the tractor, then drove it back into the barn. If the forecasts were right about the size and severity of the storm, he wouldn't be able to use it for at least a few days. Sam had heard stories of storms like this— they were overwhelming, paralyzing. So much snow fell, and so fast, that it became impossible to get hay or water to the animals. He had seen photos of livestock frozen to the ground where they stood, hunger and cold draining the life from them.

As THE MORNING progressed, and the storm drew nearer, Rose's instincts were kicking in, stirring memories and images in her mind. She pictured, in her diverse mental inventory, the hawks, raccoons, weasels, badgers, foxes, and coyotes that, if pressed by hunger, would circle the farm, probe the fence, scramble over drifts once the storm arrived.

While Sam parked the tractor, Rose lay her head on the ground, her tail curled up around her. She wondered about the old wild dog she often saw running around the woods. She wondered where he was, and what he would do in the storm.

She heard a sound out in the trees. It was not far from the barn, but Sam could not have heard it. It might have been the wild dog, or it might have been one of the coyotes that were out hunting the night before. Rose had been dreaming about them, hearing their soft footpads tracking in the night.

She lifted her nose to the flood of smells that was the world, and one that was becoming stronger. She could smell things outside even when she was in the farmhouse, and she could absorb and sift scent over great distance, through woods and storms. As scents entered her awareness, images appeared to correspond with them.

Earlier, she had caught the scent of snow on the wind, and ice, and then deer, then the old wild dog that ran through the woods, then eggs in a nest, a hundred kinds of scat, and raccoons and chickens, and the dead and frozen petals of flowers and dead leaves, and rabbits and mice. Some of the scents she caught could be miles away, and she couldn't necessarily tell how close they were, but she knew if a smell was within her range.

Now the smell was becoming clearer. It was the scent of coyote, sharp, musty, mixed with blood, fur, saliva, mud, grass, and brush—all of which flashed through her mind as images when she scented them. From the smell, she could tell the coyote was far off now and deep in the woods.

But it had come close, right across the road.

THREE

Rose knew—though Sam did not—that there was a coyote den across the road in the woods, practically in the shadow of the farmhouse.

She ran down to the road beside the farmhouse. She never stopped to look for cars or trucks, which only registered when she heard their sound. When they did get her attention, she herded or chased, then tried to run them off.

Sam was always excited and unhappy when she was near the road, yelling at her to come back, or to stop when she chased after cars and trucks. She did not understand his alarm. Rose was attuned to Sam, and obeyed almost all of his commands instantly, but this was one command she often disregarded. Her instincts overwhelmed her experience, even her judgment.

It was about midday now, and it began to snow again. Rose sensed the heavy flakes of snow before they landed on her—she could hear them falling, far up in the clouds—and began to settle on the ground. Unlike the light fine snow of the night before, these flakes were thick, wet, and they landed with a soft hiss. Rose heard them as quiet thuds, and they fell more rapidly than any she had ever seen. They began to stick to the path, and the wind began to rise, making the flakes swirl. When she had first crossed the road, she could see far down the path, but now, just a minute later, she couldn't see more than a few hundred yards.

She was headed down past the meadow, through the driving snow, into the trees.

RUNNING THROUGH THE WOODS, Rose heard raccoons and cows, and far away the barking of dogs. She also heard the wind whipping through trees, the sounds of the snow falling, the skittering of animals beneath the surface of the ground.

She heard bugs, worms, bats sighing in trees—rabbits asleep, termites gnawing, plants shrinking and changing. And beyond that—cars, trucks far off, tractors, airplanes. As she ran, she was constantly sifting and sorting the sounds, organizing them, figuring out which were close, which far, what was work, what wasn't, what mattered, what didn't. She saw all that she needed to see, little else.

The forest was a pinwheel to her, spinning sounds and sights and smells, whirling things that stimulated her. They were stories, they brought out memories, excitement, opened the vast and ancient library in her mind.

When Rose ran through the woods, often early in the morning or late at night, when Sam was asleep or busy, it was a dazzling, exciting world to her. At those times she felt alive, powerful, at peace, the colors, cries, and smells pouring through and into her, absorbing her. Rose remembered, stored, sorted. She could recall any of them in an instant, and together they made the most beautiful and intense pictures, vivid image streams of life.

Rose did not see only leaves and trees and bushes—although she saw those, too—but also too many other tales to count. She saw bright and dark colors, the glare of the sun and the cool light of the moon, and she heard the sounds of paws and hooves, the flapping of wings, the burrowing of moles and mice and chipmunks and the slithering of frogs and snakes. She heard cries, squeaks, yips, the sounds of birth, death, panic, flight, the sounds of leaves growing, dying, decaying, leaving their mark, sometimes individually, sometimes as an unremarkable mass.

ROSE WAS SEEKING the coyote, the leader of the coyotes, and she knew that he was seeking her as well. He would have known of her presence the second she crossed into the woods, and he would either be waiting or not.

An image of their first meeting flashed before Rose. It had happened when she was younger, confident in her work and strength. She had come across this coyote pup, lost and disoriented in the woods. She had stared at him, given him the eye, looked around to see if there was a mother. He had been playful, grabbing sticks, tossing them in the air, growling and running in circles, oblivious to the fact that, away from his pack, he was in danger.

Rose had seen a fox, watching up on the hill, and she had growled, stared it down, chased it off. She stood still, while the pup had drawn closer, and she had nuzzled him and led him toward the rocks where she knew the den was. It was something she had seen her mother do—to her, and to the other pups.

When the mother returned to the den, the coyote pup had run to her, then paused and looked back at Rose. That was the moment Rose and the coyote first became known to each other. After that encounter, she and the pup had an understanding. From then on, they'd cross paths in the woods several times a season.

THERE HAD BEEN that one night, well before she had found the pup in the woods. It was clear in Rose's memory, had shaped her consciousness. She remembered it often, still trying to understand it.

It had been a very different kind of day from this one, hot and sticky, with a bright sun that gave way to a nearly full moon. The moon lit up the sky and the ground, sprinkling the farm and the woods and fields with shadows. There was no breeze, the air was still, and sounds and smells moved freely and far through the night. Like most animals, Rose was always restless when the moon was large. She rarely slept on such nights.

When the moon was this big, the forest was mad with activity, the coyotes, foxes, owls, and other animals of the night signaling to one another and to the moon, in hoots, barks, and howls. Rose loved this eerie and ancient symphony, and once or twice had looked up at the moon and howled herself.

She had spent the day running in the heat, with a long tongue, and then sat down in the creek to cool herself. At night, Rose could not get comfortable in the closed-in farmhouse. On hot nights she often went to the porch, where she would hop up onto the cushion on the wicker chair and sleep, occasionally lifting her head, hoping to snare a breeze. This night, when the breeze carried the howls from the far meadows, she was almost lifted off the chair, as if hypnotized.

She left the porch, jumped over the short front fence, and headed out into the woods to follow the sounds. They were high, playful, and were almost immediately answered by howls, yips, and barks. It seemed this night that they were calling to her, and she set out to find the source.

Rose would never leave her work: There was nothing beyond the farm that was better or more important. But that night she trotted through the forest, mesmerized by the sounds, cutting through the shadows, the bushes, the moss, unnerving the owls, scattering the mice. She went on to the stream, which was shallow and easy to run across. She had never been so far from the farm without Sam's company, yet she felt no hesitation or timidity now. It felt almost like running home.

At the same time, though, the journey made her uneasy. This was not her world.

At some point, Rose slowed and went into a work crouch, listening, watching, sniffing carefully, aware of every movement and sound and smell around her. She proceeded slowly, almost at a crawl, so softly she could not hear herself. Aware of the light and shadows cast by the bright moon, her ears were back, her tail was down, her eyes were wide as an owl's. She was alert, ready to fight, freeze, or run. The sounds were near enough now that she knew precisely where they were. She was close.

She startled some rabbits, who bounded across the brush in front of her. After a little while she came to the edge of a vast, broad meadow, bounded on two sides by a creek. Nestled under a stand of tall trees, she saw what she had come to see. She was transfixed.

She moved no closer, pressing herself flat to the ground.

It was a large gathering of coyotes, several dens and their

pups scattered in a rough semicircle near the creek. There were all sizes and ages and colors, some a yellowish brown, others tawny gray, some whitish in color. Some of their tails were scraggly, some bushy; most had pointed muzzles. A few outside the circle seemed frightened, and tucked their tails between their legs, skulking at the outskirts of the group, staying near the woods.

Most had gathered right by the creek. An animal lay dead and dismembered right by the water—it smelled to Rose like a large turkey. Puppies yipped in high-pitched voices, chased one another, and stole each other's sticks and food. Mothers yipped and called for their children. Some of the males sniffed one another and the air, and looked up at the moon, barking, yipping, sometimes howling in long, piercing cries that soared across the meadow and were eaten up by the deep woods.

To Rose, they seemed carefree, joyous. Although these were strange emotions to her, she did recognize them and had seen them in some of the other animals on the farm.

She had never seen her mother play. She had seen her siblings play when she was a puppy and recognized it for what it was, but didn't grasp the point of it, or its feel. She did not hang around with other dogs. She did not relish tug-of-war or chase balls.

In the nearly full moon, glittering off the creek and lighting up the meadow, the coyotes stood out, backlit. Rose could hardly take her eyes off them.

The coyotes moved in circles, back and forth. They threw twigs in the air, raced in circles around one another, again and again, as if each one knew where to go, what to do. The older ones stayed in the center, the younger ones moved chaotically on the fringe.

Their speed was dizzying, and their howls and yips piercing and strange. Their eyes glowed, and they drooled and shook, their spittle and fur flying in the light.

It was clear to her that this was not work, and not really play either, but something old and deep and free. They tossed pieces of the dead meat into the air, and chased after them, pausing to share and roll in the scent and blood.

For the first time, she had some sense of the drama of food. Hers was given to her, but the coyotes had to find theirs, and this, more than any other thing, was what shaped the difference between her and them. She had her work, but food was *their* work.

Rose stared motionless at the group for a long time, nearly until first light, and then, backing away slowly until it was safe, turned and began the long run back to the farmhouse, the yips and howls echoing in her mind.

She was not cautious now, but free herself, sure of where she was going, unafraid of being seen, scattering the night creatures of the forest as she ran faster and faster.

It was about a year later that Rose had encountered the coyote pup on the path. After that, when she and this young coyote met in the woods, usually by chance, they didn't avoid each other as dogs and coyotes usually did. They sat and stared at each other, sometimes for minutes, then moved off. There was no fear, no aggression, no wariness between them. They had breached the wall between the two species, connected in the parts that were the same.

The coyote pup had grown, had become the leader of his den. He kept away from the farm, and kept his pack away, too. Like dogs, coyotes understood the rules and usually followed them. Even though they were feared and hunted, they understood that hunting prey in the woods—young deer, rabbits, turkey—was safer and easier than venturing near humans, fences, and dogs.

TODAY, as the storm approached, pictures rushed through Rose's mind, driving her out into the woods. In a storm like this one, there was only one rule: Survive. And there were few better survivors in the animal world than coyotes. The young leader would do what he had to do for his den, and Rose would do what she had to do to protect the farm.

They were both working creatures. Unlike the farm animals, Rose respected the coyote enough to come find him in the forest, to study him. She was curious.

Rose had heard, smelled, and seen the evidence of the coyote's work and ferocity and skill: bones and fur and signs of struggle all over the woods and paths near the farm. She understood the running tracks that suddenly stopped, and the drag marks into the forest. She saw the ability of coyotes to work together, in a way that was different from any of the other animals she knew, including dogs.

The farm animals almost never worked together, and were especially helpless against predators who did. Almost all farm animals hewed to the laws of the domestic animal—fight or flight. If they could do neither, they simply accepted their fate and perished.

When coyotes went to work, she saw, they functioned as a unit, efficiently and ruthlessly, communicated clearly through howls, barks, and yips. They killed quickly, going for the throat, dismembering, collecting pieces of their prey, hauling them off to their dens. Rose saw their stories in the sounds, smells, and tracks of the woods. Images of their lives ran through her mind.

Rose often ran with the coyotes in her mind.

As THE SNOW began to accumulate on the leaves and the upper branches of the trees, as the sky darkened, Rose came to the place where she expected the coyote to be waiting for her. She saw—sensed—well ahead of where she was that the coyote was here, and that he was aware of her. She came to a stop, seeing his eyes first. He had sensed her arrival as well.

He was sitting near a fallen tree, waiting for her, as she'd known he would be. He would have been aware from the second she came onto the path that she was coming, would have heard it and felt it through his paws. The storm had brought them both out.

Rose understood this encounter was out of the routine. In blood and memory, she was much closer to a coyote than a sheep. But her time working on the farm had honed a powerful protective instinct. The coyotes threatened the sheep. In that sense, they were a danger. Linked though they were, their lives had taken them in very different directions.

Like all dogs, she gloried in the familiar, was wary of the unusual. And she had always recognized Sam's intense reaction to coyotes. Mostly, he was unaware of them, but when he did see or hear them he seemed angry and threatened, reaching for a gun, grabbing a flashlight, scanning the woods and the pastures.

Sam reacted to the coyotes very differently than he reacted to Rose, yet she knew she could as easily have been with them as not, as easily have been outside the fence as in, looking into the house instead of sleeping and eating inside it, running from Sam instead of following him around.

This difference seemed much larger to Sam than to her. Her path led to humans, and loyalty to them. The coyotes' direction took them to one another, where their own powerful loyalties lay.

So there was an understanding, and that was why she had come.

There was already an inch of new snow on the ground and the winds were rising sharply. Rose met the coyote's eyes. They were pale yellow, luminous even in the daylight. He was large for a coyote, with a rich coat, already dusted in snow and ice.

Rose sat for a few minutes, held the coyote's gaze, and then looked away; she sniffed the air, collecting the smells and sounds of the forest. Off in the woods, she heard other coyotes, deep in their dens, scratching, snuffling. She felt the power of the storm drawing closer.

Strong instincts had brought her out into the woods. The coyote pup, the gathering in the far meadow, the presence of this coyote in the shadow of the farm. All of these things had entered her consciousness, defined in an elemental way what she was, and what she wasn't.

She had not come for human reasons: to warn or threaten, to feel good or bad or happy or sad. She came because it was in her blood to acknowledge that the storm would change her understanding with the coyote, their awareness of each other, the curious connection that defined their parallel existences.

The storm brought into focus that he mattered. And she did not forget what was important, or let go of it easily. She would do her work. He would do his. Everything would be different.

He looked away as well, then back to her. Then he stood

and trotted off, his body fusing with the snow, before vanishing. Soon Rose could not hear him.

A MOMENT LATER, Rose lifted herself from her haunches and began to head back through the wind and swirling white. The snow was starting to pile up now and small balls of ice were gathering on her legs.

She felt excitement—the glorious arousal of work. She felt fear, the awful spectre of failure to accomplish a task, as embedded in her genes as life itself. She felt obligation to Sam, to protect him and to protect the farm. And she felt love. For Sam, for Katie, even for the sheep, the other animals, and the farm itself, under her care, within her boundaries.

She came within sight of the farm and took in the world around her, through the snow. She called up her map, her inventory, her life—

The sheep in the pole barn beginning to huddle. The fences, the gates.

The cows in the back pasture gathering in the shed.

The goats, loud and restless in their pen.

The rooster and chickens back in the barn.

Her responsibility, to all of them, to get them through, to help Sam, to grasp his meaning and be of service to him.

SHE TURNED BACK for a moment and looked down the path, as ever alert for signs of Katie, who often walked there. She knew Katie was not in the woods that day, for she had just run through them.

But she always looked.

FOUR

ABOUT HALFWAY BACK TO THE FARMHOUSE, ROSE DETOURED slightly to the big stump at the edge of a meadow a little more than halfway back on the path toward the farm. It was already covered in a thin layer of snow. Heavy flakes were blowing into Rose's eyes, and the wind was building to a steady roar. But Rose turned and went over to it anyway, touching the stump with her nose, and listening.

Katie used to wait for Rose here. She would be sitting on the old oak stump and would always have a piece of bread for her.

But today there was no bread, and no Katie.

Rose pointed her nose in several different directions, tilted her ears, raised her head, listened, then stopped, sat, sniffed. Perhaps Katie would appear. Rose had no way of measuring time, except as a sequence of darkness and light. She had no awareness of how long it had been since she had last seen Katie.

* * *

SAM WASN'T MUCH for nostalgia, but he loved to remember—
and tell—the story about when Katie had first come to the
farm. He had watched as Katie, tall and thin with long dark-
brown hair, had come up to Rose and tried to pet her. Sam had
warned her that Rose, then three years old and set in her ways,
did not like to be touched, or even approached by people other
than him. He was right—when Katie extended her hand to
the dog, she growled and nipped, as he'd predicted. Startled,
Katie pulled her hand away.

But Sam was impressed by what happened next. Katie
calmly stepped back, looking curiously at Rose, who lowered
her ears and backed away, too.

Sam reprimanded Rose sharply, then grabbed a boot lying
on the floor and threw it at her. Dog training farmer-style, as
his father had taught him.

Rose had been surprised, abashed, as he rarely corrected
her, or had reason to. But Sam believed there was a point in the
life of any dog—of any animal, for that matter—where authority had to be clearly and forcefully established once and for
all. Otherwise there would always be trouble.

This was something he would not and could not abide. She
had to learn that. Rose was a strong dog, and sometimes she
needed strong direction. Sam never hesitated to provide it.

"She's a good dog, a great dog, but she's a working dog."
Sam explained to Katie that working dogs are not really pets;
they don't always like or want to be cuddled or petted. "She
stays focused. It's her farm," he said, adding that Rose had little use for things that didn't involve work, not even treats or
toys.

Pushing sheep and cows around was not gentle or easy
work, he said. The animals did not like to be pushed around by
a dog.

She was not, he said, cute.

Rose was always looking for work, which was the key to her heart. She loved people who gave her work, or worked with her. "Every once in a while," Sam explained, "she'll hop up on the sofa next to me, and let me scratch her belly, but not very often. And she won't do it for anyone else."

Sam had watched as Katie looked at Rose, meeting her gaze with a smile. "Well, we have a challenge here," she said, and he could tell that Rose understood that Katie was not afraid of her. The dog seemed to look at her with renewed interest.

ABOUT A YEAR LATER, and after many visits, Katie had come to live on the farm. Rose's map as well as her life was thrown into chaos, her rhythms and routines upset and confused. This woman made her nervous. She didn't go away, and she came with new things—furniture, clothes, new smells. She talked to Sam constantly, and spent too much time with him.

Rose kept waiting for her to leave again, as all the other people did.

Rose had been alone with Sam for most of her life in the farmhouse. Katie had nothing to do with work or sheep, at least not that Rose could see.

But Katie was now in Sam's bedroom at night, and so Rose no longer hopped up onto the bed to check on him as she sometimes used to do. Once in a while Katie fed her, but Rose would refuse to eat from the bowl she put down. Rose only ate when Sam fed her.

Sometimes, she would look up to see Katie looking at her, watching her, smiling at her, and when Sam was not around, Rose would lower her ears, look away, even growl, trying to get her to go. But Katie did not leave, and her sounds and smells and voice began to be part of the farmhouse. They were slowly added to Rose's ever-evolving map, becoming part of the image of the place. If Katie was with Sam, then she was part of Rose's work. That made her different from other humans.

Katie did not touch Rose again, and Rose eventually stopped growling at her. She got used to her gradually, her soft and quiet voice. Rose loved routine, patterns, and even though it seemed like an annoying distraction, she was getting used to Katie's presence.

Rose PAID close attention to shoes, and what kind Sam was wearing at any given moment told her if they were going to work. One day Sam left the farm, and Rose noticed that Katie was wearing the same kind of boots Sam wore when he went into the pasture or the barns. They had sheep manure on them. Rose looked at Katie eagerly, and her instincts were confirmed when Katie said, "Rose, let's go to work." Rose barked and rushed to the back door.

She ran to the pasture gate and waited as Katie, a little uncertainly, opened it. Rose tore up the hill to the pole barn, and, as the sheep gathered themselves into a circle, she made an outrun behind them and started moving them back and forth, pushing them down to the hay feeders. She never let the sheep rush toward Sam, nor would she now with Katie.

When the sheep were at the feeders, Rose sensed something was wrong. Katie was gone. She heard the sound of the back door of the barn opening, and then a grain bucket scraping along the ground. She heard the cows and steers moving quickly—too quickly—in the other pasture, on the other side of the barn. A picture came into her head of Katie hauling a grain bucket out to the cows. The image was wrong.

Cows and steers could be excitable around grain. Sam always had Rose push the steers and cows into a holding pen and keep them there while he closed the heavy gate and put the grain out, then he came back and opened the gate to let them run to the troughs. It was a potentially dangerous situation, especially for someone who seemed anxious and confused— Rose understood the importance of appearing confident and decisive, no matter what. The animals believed she was in charge, so she was.

Some of the steers weighed more than two thousand pounds and could easily crush or trample a person. Sam was never around these animals without Rose. When the dog saw that Katie was out in the pasture alone with them and a grain bucket, it was so different from the way Sam did it that it drew her attention and set off an alarm.

She left the sheep and rushed around the corner and into the open door of the barn. She was running fast now, right past Winston, who clucked and huffed in surprise. Rose came rocketing out the other side. She saw that in the middle of the pasture, holding a grain bucket, trudging to the trough— seemingly unaware of two steers and five cows closing in on her from behind—was Katie.

Cows should not be moving that fast, should never be that excited, never get so close to people. It was not yet a stampede, but it could become one at any moment.

Rose barked and saw Katie's head turn. Then she ran out in front of the steers and cows, who were starting to build up a head of steam. She darted close to Brownie, the largest steer, nipping him on the nose, surprising and distracting him. She

circled around, and leapt up and bit his tail, causing him to bellow and turn, slowing the animals behind him.

Surprised, Katie shouted in alarm. She reacted quickly,
throwing the bucket away, the grain spilling to the ground,
and then walking fast toward the open door of the barn.

Brownie lowered his huge head to swing at Rose, but she
was well back, circling and nipping. After a moment, she ran
over to join Katie in the barn, and the door swung shut. The
two of them stood there with Winston and the chickens in the
dark corner of the barn, hay stacked all around them.

Katie's eyes were wide, and she was breathing heavily. She
had a hand on her heart. Rose sat down, and Katie looked at
her.

"What are you thinking? That I'm foolish?"

Rose tilted her head, so that her ears could more easily absorb this sound, and she puzzled over the tone of voice. It was
not a command, or a reproach, but the tone made her curious.

Katie sank down onto a bale of hay, and for once Rose did
not back off or growl, but stayed close, meeting her gaze.

"Thank you, Rose," Katie said softly, a new tone of voice.
Rose recognized it as affectionate, a tone of praise and appreciation she sometimes heard from Sam.

She knew what Katie was trying to communicate, and for
the first time, her tail wagged and she let Katie reach out to pet
her, licking her hand two or three times. But she withdrew before Katie could touch her.

"Well, well," Katie said. "So Sam was right. Once some-
body works with you, then they have a purpose in this world,
huh?"

* * *

Now, A POWERFUL GUST of wind blew snow and ice into Rose's face, and she shook it off, brought sharply back into the present. She felt the wind, and a numbness in her paws, which was rare. There was a chill that ran down her spine and caused her to shake, as if it were summer and Sam had turned the hose on her.

She turned from the stump and began to trot homeward.

FIVE

When Rose emerged from the woods and approached the road in front of the farm, she found it completely covered in snow. Since she had left the farm, a vicious squall had set in, and it was more obvious once she was outside the cover of trees. The snow was now falling more heavily than she had ever seen it. It was already deep enough that it was brushing the fur on her belly.

She imagined the sheep and other animals beginning to panic, not because the snow was that deep, but because it was falling so thickly that it had become like a wall, surrounding everything. The farm animals had not seen such snow or wind before and Rose knew that nothing frightened animals more than what was new.

As she neared the farmhouse, she heard Sam shouting before she saw him through the blowing snow, up on the hill behind the farmhouse. She quickened her pace. As she got closer, she could sense his worry.

* * *

SAM'S VOICE WAS sharp and rising. "Rose! Rose, where are you?" He followed the call with a piercing whistle, his other signal.

Sam knew Rose made occasional forays off into the woods, and he had never thought much about it. But when he called her, he expected her to be there, and most often she was.

He saw her as she approached and figured out right away what was wrong.

The goats had indeed panicked as the snow thickened and the terrifying winds rose with a howl, like a great predator materializing out of the air itself, blowing one of the feeders right through part of their fencing. In their fear, they had crawled over it and through the gaping hole in the fence, then taken off up the hill.

Sam pointed to the cow pasture. He often communicated to Rose through pointing, which he knew she understood. Rose followed his arm with her eyes, took in what he was pointing to.

"Look," he said. And she did.

It was in these moments that his feeling for Rose mushroomed inside of him, sometimes nearly overwhelmed him. He thought Rose could probably sense what he didn't say: We'll figure this out together.

The cows had panicked as well, but most of them ran toward the barn, which they could see. The sheep had all retreated into the pole barn, where they huddled together. A small group of beef cows, though, had separated from the rest of the herd by the snow, blinded by the sudden squall, and, alarmed by the shrieking wind, had run, breaking through one of the gates and heading up to the top of the hill to take shelter under a stand of trees.

Even though the trees were now bare and the site exposed

to the storm, this is where the cows always went during rain and thunderstorms if the gate was left open. It represented safety to them, shelter, a familiar place to go when they were confused. A place they knew was there, even though they couldn't see very far in front of them.

Sam had to shout through the rising wind.

"Rose, we have to find the goats, get them in. Then we have to get the cows in," he said, pointing up to the top of the hill. "Anybody left out in this will be in trouble."

Sam expected the paths and pastures to soon be impassable. The winds were so fierce, and the temperature plummeting so sharply, he doubted that any farm animal would survive long out in the open. He wondered if the hardier outdoor animals like deer and rabbits would make it. Although Sam and the other farmers usually paid little attention to the weather forecasters and their overheated predictions, he thought this time they might have greatly underestimated the storm.

He saw Rose focus. She paused, then tore through the snow, under the gate and up the hill. She was used to unexpected crises.

Few of the farmers in the county had working dogs; as Sam had, they assumed they'd take too much time and trouble to train. And they cost money. So as Rose's reputation had spread, Sam often got calls in the middle of the night from other farmers asking for Rose—cows in the road, stray dogs, sheep scattered in pastures, rioting goats.

"Rose, we've got a farm emergency," Sam would say, smiling, and the two of them would roar off in Sam's pickup to clear things up. Sam loved these journeys, when he got to show off Rose and help a pal out.

When Sam called for her in the night, opening the door of the truck, she'd bark and spin for joy, leaping onto the front seat across from Sam. She was always ready to go. And she always delivered, getting cows back in the barns, rounding up stray or lost sheep.

Sam didn't like to take money from the grateful farmers, but he didn't want to insult them either. They had great pride, most of them. So he charged ten dollars per visit. He put the money in a basket in the living room, and whenever Rose's "emergency pot" hit thirty dollars he would go to the basement, pull out a frozen steak, and grill a big chunk for Rose's dinner.

Sam and the other farmers always marveled at Rose's gift for problem solving, her ability to gauge a situation and respond to it. Her routine never varied. She'd get out of the truck, look around, adjust her map, then get to work. She was like a Texas Ranger, he used to tell the other farmers. One riot, one dog.

There was the night a stray dog chased Kay Crank's sheep up into the hills around Hebron. Rose went up into the woods and brought them back. And there was the night Roland Hanks's cows walked right through his single-strand homemade wire fence and onto Route 22, a busy state highway filled with speeding trucks and cars. That was dangerous, Sam recalled, as the farm's animals were milling in the road—hard to see at night—and Rose couldn't round them up without darting onto the road herself.

Hanks, joked Sam, would never stop talking about how Rose jumped out of the truck, ran the cows into the barn, chased off the hysterical and useless farm dogs, and restored order in minutes. Hanks offered to buy her on the spot, but Sam said she wasn't for sale.

Sam felt vindicated, as many farmers liked to ridicule people who paid money for dogs.

* * *

TODAY, the farm had its own emergency.

Rose lifted her nose, raised her eyes, tilted her ears, followed the tracks. She knew right away where the goats would be—up over the crest of the hill and out of sight, foraging for bark and brush, or hiding from the wind. She could almost *feel* where they were.

She looked at Sam, who was trying to clear some snow away from the goat pen, and then took off up the hill, through the snow, running and leaping, and plowing through where she had to. It took her a couple of minutes, but soon she crested the hill, reaching a point from which she could no longer see Sam below.

There, off into the woods on her left, were the three goats, nibbling on the lower branches of some pine trees. They baaed and stirred when they saw her, but Rose knew that goats, unlike sheep, were not flocking animals, nor did they care to be herded. And they neither liked nor feared dogs. Goats were wont to challenge a dog.

Rose could not manage them with her eyes the way she could the sheep, nor startle them easily like cows. They were smart and stubborn, and they didn't mind fighting, either, quick to lower their heads and butt, or kick out with their sharp hooves.

Rose moved around the pine stand to get behind the goats and cut off any flight into the woods, where it might be impossible to push them back out. She had an innate sense of how animals would move, and was always ahead of them in sensing their possible directions. If they broke, Rose was usually waiting for them.

In her work, Rose was always mindful of Sam, always

knew where he was, and always tried to keep whatever animals she was working between her and him.

Watching her warily, the three goats kept nibbling, almost frantically, on the bark and twigs. Rose crept up behind them until she was a few feet away. She saw they were unnerved by the shrieking wind and by the snow blowing into their eyes, and she worried they might bolt. She sat down and watched, trying to work out how she might move them.

After a moment, she charged at the goat closest to her, the leader. He turned, then lowered his head quickly and butted her, cracking her on the side of the nose. She yelped, and leapt back.

He was faster than she had anticipated.

She paused again, took in the scene, and then moved to the left, shaking off the pain near her eye. She ran alongside his tail and nipped at his side, and as he spun, she bit his haunches. He spun twice, then lowered his head.

The spinning had confused him a bit, Rose saw. She did it again. Then again. He looked less certain now, less aggressive.

One of the other goats lowered her head to butt Rose, but waited, cautious about engaging her. Rose gave her the eye, a strong warning look. The third kept eating, watching her nervously. Goats did not act in unison, but Rose knew that these were very attached to one another, and they hated to be alone. They would stay close.

If she could get one to move, the others should follow. She kept an eye on all of them and didn't allow herself to be surrounded. Goats had little patience and short attention spans. That was their weakness.

Rose had lots of patience, and she never quit.

She backed up, lowered her head, and began barking and

growling. Every few seconds, when the male began to nibble on the bark, she would charge at him and bite his shoulder, then spin him again. He was tiring of this. He would rather be eating hay—anywhere—than trying to outmaneuver this determined creature. Rose grasped this. She had to wear him down. He would quit. She wouldn't.

The other two were bleating loudly, anxious. She stopped, lowered her head, bared her teeth, barked more insistently. The male came out again to charge at her, but she was well prepared for him now, and he would not get close enough to butt her again. She sidestepped him and turned suddenly, going after the younger female, the most timid of the three.

That goat cried out, and Rose, making sure she was between her and the shed, leapt forward and bit her on the nose, drawing blood. It was a sensitive spot, and it moved sheep rapidly, but it stunned the younger goat, frightened her. The goat turned, complaining in a loud and shrill way, and then began running in retreat down the hill.

The other two lifted their heads in confusion, and Rose got behind them and lunged and barked and nipped. She had them. Rose kept at it for a few minutes, and, as she knew would happen, they eventually quit the struggle and tore off after their mate down the hill, toward the safety of Sam, whom they associated with food and the shed that was their shelter.

They bounded nimbly through the snow over the hilltop, faster than Rose could run through such deep drifts, down to the shed. Sam held the gate open and Rose made her way, steadily and laboriously, down the hill after them, to make sure they felt her silent pressure at their backs.

Sam closed the gate and, that done, looked up at the renegade cows. Without additional conversation or commands,

Rose veered off across the pasture and into the stand of trees where the cows were clustered, mooing and huddling together for warmth, trying unsuccessfully to get out of the wind and snow.

Rose could see that they needed to get down into the lower pasture as the wind was ferocious at the hilltop. She could already feel the warmth draining from her own body.

Rose went into a crouch and lay still, watching as Sam made his way through the storm to the lower cow pasture, where he shoveled for a few minutes to make sure the gate was clear. It had been forced open a few feet by the wind-spooked animals, and that was where these cows would have gotten out.

Rose pursued a different strategy with the cows. Though they were more pliant, cows were also more dangerous than goats, especially when they panicked. Cows could kill a dog with one kick, crack her skull, or trample her. She had been kicked a few times, and she remembered it well. Still, cows were also dumber and slower and much more predictable.

She lay low to the ground, creeping along slowly. One or two of the cows had noticed her and bellowed, but when she stopped moving, she lost their interest again. Rose waited until Sam had the gate cleared. When he waved his hand and called out to her, her ears tilted to pick up his voice cutting through the roaring wind and snow. "Rose, get the cows here."

She moved up two or three feet, then stopped. The cows, sensing her movement, became more anxious now, stirring. She eased forward, then paused again. More bellowing, a bit more confusion. She darted to the left, above the cows, keeping them between her and Sam, as always.

But she suddenly realized the flaw in her plan: They might

run farther up the hill, or to the other side of the pasture since they could move through snow more easily than she could. If they did, it would be difficult to get them back across that distance.

Rose watched them carefully, reading them, studying them. She thought, in her own way, of a triangle. Sam was below, she was above. In her mind, she chose to put pressure on them to move down, while she made sure to flank them on the left and keep them from going off to the side.

She zigzagged down and to the left, like a sailboat tacking in the wind. The group moved up a bit, away from Sam, so she changed position, went into an outrun, swung away wide and farther up the hill.

They stopped moving, shifted back to the shelter of the stand. Rose crept slowly down the hill, Sam no longer visible in the snow. She waited some time, then padded forward again, as slowly and quietly as she could. Soon she was within a few feet of the cows, which did not know where she was or notice her. She could tell that by their silence.

Then she leapt forward, bursting out of the bushes above the cows, plowing through a string of icicles and sending them crashing to the ground. Landing right under one of the smaller cows, she jumped up and bit her on the underside, making enough noise and commotion in the process for the cows to think she was a pack.

The cows were duly frightened and confused. They bolted and bellowed in alarm. They fled the trees and started down the hill, Rose in close pursuit, barking, veering to the left and then back, giving the animals in the rear no opportunity to pause or turn around. She moved so rapidly, it was as if she really were a pack.

Soon the cows' own momentum was carrying them on-ward to familiar ground, and they came rumbling down the hill, slowed only by the snow and biting wind in their faces.

Sam had thrown some hay out onto the ground, and in a few minutes, the cows were back in the pasture and the gate was closed. Satisfied, Rose and Sam began their walk back through the barn to the farmhouse.

"Good girl," he said, appreciative, but also focused on other things. There was still much to do to get the farm ready for the worst of the storm.

He did lean over and look at her head. Her tongue was long, and she was panting. Her eye was slightly swollen from the goat-butting. The cows had not touched or harmed her, and she had moved them easily enough.

"You're okay," he said.

An hour later, Sam ventured back out to the barn to try to get his spare generator, broken for more than a year, working again, and also to haul more hay to the animals and see if he couldn't keep the paths clear.

While she waited for him, Rose lay down in the snow and wind, and, briefly, closed her eyes.

SIX

BY LATE AFTERNOON, IN THE FADING LIGHT, DRIFTS WERE beginning to pile up around the walls and tree trunks and ridges in the ground, and the gusts were so strong they nearly blew Rose off her feet.

She looked up at the altered landscape, and there was nothing in her memory like it. The farm was at the edge of a valley, wide and open fields for miles, ringed by rolling hills and one or two mountains. None of that was visible now. Rose's world was blue and white, snow whirling up and down across the pastures, the wind a steady roar now, mist steaming up from the hills as the temperature continued to plunge.

The wind was disorienting to her. Because of it, everything was moving—snow, tree limbs, drifts—and the roar of the air made it difficult for her to sort out sounds. Still, her senses were gradually adapting, separating the movement of the storm from the things living within it.

Rose caught a strange scent on the wind. She raised her head, then felt, rather than saw, an animal near the barn that did not belong there. That was not unusual. There were al-

most always animals of one kind or another for her to keep
track of. But as she went to check on the sheep, she picked up
a scent of dog, familiar, but closer than usual. She recognized
it, and focused on the smell. It was within her territory.

Now she heard it moving. It was large, but it wasn't the
coyote, nor any other coyote—not before nightfall, not in the
storm, not so close.

Rose, moving behind the farmhouse, had to turn her head
out of the wind. The snow was blinding now and she needed
to leap over the larger drifts.

Today she was not surprised, as she might normally have
been, to look through the curtain of white and see the old wild
dog, sitting by the big barn, patiently, calmly, his coat covered
with snow.

The dog was looking right at Rose, but it was not a challenge, as such looks between dogs often are. His look was plain
to her: The wild dog was seeking shelter, asking to come in
from the storm. And he was waiting for permission, as a gesture of deference and respect to her. He wouldn't proceed
without her agreement.

He conveyed to Rose—she saw it in his eyes, body posture,
scent, tail, and shoulders—that he could not survive this storm
out in the woods. That he was tired, weakening.

Rose's eyes met his and she froze for nearly a full minute.
Fifty yards separated them, the snow and wind swirling about
them. It was up to her. One kind of look and he would vanish
into the maelstrom, the wind and the drifts, not be seen again.
Another and he would follow her where she led him. She could
drive the wild dog away with a mere change in posture. He was
signaling to her that he would accept this by not advancing, and
looking away dropping his shoulders, lowering his tail and ears.

She could accept his presence, and bring him into the barn,

where it would be safe and dry, and where the dog could find shelter and, perhaps, some food. A number of images raced through her mind. Would the chickens and rooster and the sheep be safe?

For a minute, the wild dog was obscured by blowing snow. When it cleared, she searched his eyes again.

She knew this dog. He had never been on the farm, yet his smell and presence had been known to her for a long time. He was not a threat to the animals. He was emaciated, she could see, his ribs protruding, his eyes bloodshot, his fur matted with ice and twigs and brush. His breath was weak, irregular. The wild dog was no longer a predator, but was now, she saw, prey, especially for the coyotes, out in the woods. Crippled and alone, he could not run fast or fight hard. Rose understood that she was communicating with an animal near the end of his life, his spirit draining.

She relaxed her shoulders and ears. He could take shelter here.

He would not challenge her, or harm or seek food from the other animals. He could not move freely about the farm. She could not protect him from humans or predators. This was all understood.

He returned the gaze, then lowered his head, looking away. He had accepted. Rose, increasingly blinded by the wind and battered by the pelting sharp snow—and feeling, uncharacteristically for her, the sting of bitter cold—led the wild dog to the rear pasture gate. There she jumped over the snowdrift, already halfway up to the top of the fence there.

The wild dog, head down, followed her slowly. Rose felt his presence behind her and sensed his struggle. She hopped down the other side, and he made his way carefully, slipping, nearly falling, several times.

Rose went ahead, saw the sheep stir, reacting to the sight of a strange dog—she held them in place with a look—and then she and the wild dog entered through the open side door of the barn. The wild dog followed Rose inside as she surveyed the space. The chickens fled to the rear of the barn, and the two barn cats came hissing down out of the rafters, keeping their distance, showing their contempt for Rose and the new dog, then slinking away. Rose ignored them, as did the wild dog.

Up the hill, the goats were bleating in alarm at his sight and smell. He followed Rose toward the rear of the barn, below the circling cats, where the cow feed was stored, past Winston the rooster, who feared no dog.

Winston, Rose saw, held his ground in part to protect the hens. He took a look at the wild dog, and then at Rose, who was calm, and he seemed to grasp what was happening. Rose was startled when Brownie stuck his huge head through the open barn window. Steers were not usually interested in dogs who were not interested in them.

Rose and the wild dog made their way to the wooden plank that covered the grain bin but which was rarely closed all the way. The wild dog clambered up, stuck his nose through the opening, and ate hungrily, pausing to look at Rose and to make sure of her continued permission. Rose watched him eat for several minutes. Then, sated, he crawled to a pile of hay, where he lay down and closed his eyes.

Once he was asleep, the animals around him, Rose sensed, accepted his presence and moved on. The barn was dark and quiet. The chickens hobbled back to their warm roosts, with Winston following, and Rose watching over them all.

* * *

Sam had once known him as "Flash," but now called him "that wild dog," and Rose connected him to that name. She had halfheartedly chased this dog away from the farm so many times that it was just another chore to her. Until now, he had never come near the house or animals, which was curious to her. Most stray dogs tried to get close to the barns, to the chickens, to food. But he always watched from the safety of the woods, and all it took was a look or bark or growl to make him vanish.

She'd never considered the old dog a threat, and she had never really seen him up close. Still, there was something about him that drew her, some cloudy connection—an air of dominance, dignity, a posture that suggested authority and strength. He seemed careful to defer to her here, yet there was something uncomfortable about that role. He was puzzling.

But apart from chasing him off, as she did deer and raccoons and other stray dogs, she'd had no reason to consider this animal much until now. What was beyond the fences of the farm was another world, something of curiosity, but not of importance since it was not her work.

Sam, however, did have reason to consider this dog more carefully. It was, for him, a personal story, because the dog had belonged to his friend Harold McEachron. Harold had run a hundred-head dairy farm a couple of miles away in the valley, and he and Sam worked some rental acreage together, planted and plowed the land, shared equipment, traded gossip, hard-luck stories, and news of farm life. Harold was tough, and a tough negotiator. But he was also fair and honest.

This dog was a working dog when Sam first knew him,

just like Rose. A border collie/shepherd mix, smart, aggressive with other dogs, shy of most people. He was tough and tireless, and he herded cattle and sheep and rode around with his farmer on his tractor half the day.

Like Sam, Harold didn't have much time for dog training, or much interest in it. Animals had to work to pay their way, or take their own chances. But Harold loved his dog in the same way that Sam loved Rose, and the two were inseparable.

Sam remembered the funeral. Harold McEachron and his wife, both killed in a car accident five years earlier. He had wondered about the dog, talked about him with McEachron's sons. No one was living at the farm, the livestock tended by neighboring farmers while the couple's sons decided what to do with the place. Flash had always slept outside in the barns, even in winter, and he wouldn't come near the house after Harold died, wouldn't let anyone come near him.

The sons had come by the farm for days, calling to him, trying to lure him in, but they said the dog had become hostile, almost feral, living on his own, scavenging garbage, hunting for rabbits and chickens. Knowing how much Harold had loved the dog, Sam sometimes, when he had a free moment, would drive his truck around in the woods on logging trails and fire roads and call for him. But he was never able to catch him, or even get close.

In the months that followed, the dog was seen from time to time in the woods and pastures around Harold's farm. Sam had left some food out for him a couple of times, and it was usually gone in the morning, but he never knew if it was the dog that ate it, and he knew it was bad practice to leave food out near a farm as it attracted foxes and coyotes, and mice and rats as well. After a while, he stopped, and it seemed that the dog became increasingly wild, his sightings rare and farther away. Sam hated to think of this loyal dog out in the winter, foraging for food in the bitter cold.

The wild dog had become almost a kind of local myth, seen everywhere, too wily to catch. After a couple of years, the family decided to sell the farm, and Sam came by to help them close the place up and get it ready to show. Sam was surprised to see the old working dog running out in the pasture. It happened only once, and that was when Harold McEachron's tractor was turned on.

Harold's children moved away—the farm was too full of painful reminders for them—and never returned. The wild dog became just another wild animal in the woods, like the coyotes or bobcats or deer. He was no longer the kind of animal a farmer would tolerate around a farm. Besides, the dog was determined to stay in the woods, and that was his choice. It had happened to working dogs before, Sam knew, loyal to an owner beyond reason or change. He often wondered what Rose would do if anything happened to him. God help the person who tried to catch her.

In the past year or so, Sam had noticed the wild dog hanging around the woods near his own farm. Rose had barked at him several times. To Sam, he was just another wild animal now, a potential source of disease and trouble, a threat to the farm.

Once when Sam spotted him in the near woods where the hens foraged for bugs, he grabbed the .30-06 and took a few shots into the air above him, aiming to scare him off—not kill him—and the dog did run off, at least out of sight. Sam thought of his old friend with some regret, but knew Harold would understand that he had no choice.

Now the wild dog lived more like a coyote than a dog, Sam thought. According to the few people who had gotten close enough to see him, he limped badly and had all kinds of injuries—scars from battles with raccoons, coyotes, and other dogs.

Now Sam heard a commotion coming from the barn. Like most farmers, he had a sense of the familiar, an intuition a little like Rose's map. Farms are intimate, personal places, bounded by rhythmic chores, sights, and sounds. Sam knew every inch of his.

Everything on the place—the old buildings, scraggly fences, troughs, rusting engines, animals, swinging gates, wind whistling through barn walls—had a distinctive sound to him. Morning sounded one way, night another. Safe and contented animals made one kind of noise, hungry and disturbed ones another.

Like Rose, Sam often sensed rather than saw or heard things, and when he noticed the excited clucking of the chickens, the clamoring of the goats, he understood something different was happening, that something was out of place.

He looked out the window, peered through the snow, and saw the sheep backing up nervously into the pole barn.

And he didn't see Rose. Or hear her bark.

He put on his jacket and boots and walked through the snow and wind and cold to the barn. It was the only place Rose could be. If something had bothered the chickens, surely she would investigate. But by now everything was quiet again.

Sam stumbled in the icy snow, recovered, and shook his head. The brute force of the wind and cold and the mounting snow suggested that for once weather forecasters' hysteria might be warranted.

Sam unlatched the gate, slid open the barn door, and

turned on the single bare bulb that lit up the cavernous, dusty barn. He stopped. He saw Rose move over to what at first appeared to be a dead dog lying on the ground. The dog lifted his head, then lowered it again warily.

"The wild dog," he said softly. It pierced his heart to see this battered creature, Harold McEachron's old border collie mix—for so many years a shadow in the woods, a rumor— now lying in his barn.

"You look a wreck," he said. "But you can't stay in here, old boy." The words came spilling out of his mouth, a farmer's reflex. Almost anything from outside the fences was a potential danger or problem. It was never a simple thing to bring a new animal onto a farm, especially a wild dog into the midst of chickens and sheep.

He was amazed that Rose had allowed it.

Sam took a few steps toward the dog, who growled, quietly but clearly, and then stopped. Rose lay still, almost stiff. She rarely looked into Sam's eyes and he was startled to see her looking into his eyes now.

"You let him in, didn't you?"

Rose did not move.

The last thing he needed was another animal now, let alone a sick old dog. He tried to figure out what had happened; normally Rose chased strays off and would have prevented any dog from coming onto the property. Now she was lying next to Harold's old dog, Flash, a dog Sam had pretty much given up for dead.

"Rose," he said, quietly.

She lay still, but looked away. The wild dog remained still as well, his eyes closed, his stomach heaving gently. It was clear he was spent.

Sam took a deep breath. He might not have a lot of time to

think about things, but when he did, it was carefully. He looked at this loyal dog, and felt he owed this to Rose. It was her farm, too. He thought of her dignity, here in the barn, in front of the animals, and her pride. She had never asked a thing of him, and gave so much, every day of her life.

It was dark in the barn, even with the bare bulb, and they were all cast in flickering shadow. The barn was rich in smells—hay, manure, dirt, animals. The wind was shrieking outside, and piercing the slats in the walls. Inside, the cold was tolerable, but still biting.

Sam left the barn and walked back toward the house. In a few minutes, he reappeared with a large bowl of dog food and put it on the floor near the old dog.

"See you in the house," he said to Rose, and left again. Outside, night had fallen, and the snow swirled through blackness.

SEVEN

THAT NIGHT, ROSE WAS UNEASY, PACING THE HOUSE. Occasionally she walked over to the bedroom window upstairs, the one that faced the pasture. A few feet away Sam slept
fitfully in the big bed. By midnight, the snow was piled up to
the lower windowpanes downstairs, and Rose could no longer
see the sheep, although she could make out the dark outline of
the barn.

She heard the wind, the snow falling, the bellow of a cow
or the call of an anxious ewe. Then she heard another sound,
faint, but to her distinct. There were squawks coming from
the barn. Chickens almost never make noise at night, sound
sleepers up in their roosts. And this was a sound of alarm.

There were things for which she awakened Sam—a ewe
in labor, animals out of the fences—and things she did not,
things that were her work alone. This time she did not bark
for Sam.

She tore out the back door and raced through the snow.

She could hear what was happening, piecing it together
from the noise a bit more with each step. She heard the yip-yip

of a fox, the crowing of Winston, the rapid, excited clucking of the hens.

The drifts had grown since she'd come inside earlier that evening. She dove over and through them, scrambling and clawing her way to the gate, and then squirmed under it. She threw herself through the open side door of the barn and into the dimly lit space, where she was greeted by chaos. The cats were nowhere to be seen. There were feathers on the barn floor, and tracks and blood in the snow and ice on the cement.

At first, it seemed she was too late. She saw where a fox must have slipped in, through a wind-shattered window above the chicken roost. At the rear of the barn, which was built into an incline, the ground came up nearly to the windows, and the snow would have made it easy for the fox to get the rest of the way. It was a savvy way to get at the chickens without coming through the main doors of the barn.

Winston, she saw, would have been the first to see the fox creep along the platform, around the old hay bales, toward the chicken coop. Winston would have darted in front of the hens, one of which had panicked and rushed across to try to hide in a corner. That was where Rose found the fox, stalking the hen. Rose sensed other foxes must be nearby, waiting for a signal from this one. That was what the yipping had been—a signal.

Rose heard the wild dog barking, circling, and she could see him struggling, limping, unable to jump. He was weak and confused. The fox—poised—was watching him, sizing him up, but he did not run. The wild dog was no threat.

As always, a strategy came instantly to Rose's mind.

Winston was desperately trying to draw the fox off and distract him by puffing himself up and crowing as loudly as he could. The wild dog was barking, but could not get close.

The fox, who could have easily killed Winston, was not

distracted or fooled. He was down in a crouch, ready to strike, to grab the hen by the throat and carry her up and out through the nearby window. Winston puffed up his wings again and prepared to charge the fox, to sacrifice himself, if necessary.

Rose hesitated and thought of Sam, of sounding the alarm. Part of her work was to alert him when there was trouble. But there was no time to get him. If she left the barn, she knew that the fox, gray and sleek, efficient and quick, would soon be long gone, at least one hen along with him. So she stayed.

Rose moved quickly but calmly across the barn floor, jumped up onto a hay bale and onto the platform that supported the roost. She glanced at the wild dog, keeping him back. It wasn't necessary. She knew he could not jump or fight, and his barking would help unnerve, perhaps even distract, the fox.

Rose barked, went into a crouch, showed her teeth, and jumped onto a feed sack to gain height, and then charged across the dark, wooden floor. The roosts were between her and the fox, momentarily blocking his view of her.

Then she whirled around and faced him.

The fox, momentarily uncertain, spun but held his ground, a hen circling in panic behind him. The fox was alert and low, with bright blue-gray eyes. And he was very calm, looking Rose in the eye, considering her, gauging his situation. Rose saw that he was not afraid of her.

Winston rushed around her to get himself in front of the hen, to make a last stand, if necessary. Rose imagined the fox snapping this officious bird in two, however gallant he was.

She moved closer, matching the fox's cool with her own, an old and ritualistic dance. It was a test of nerves and strategy, not necessarily strength and power. She would use her eyes— her keenest weapon—as well as her teeth. Rose always battled bigger and stronger creatures. Her eyes caused them to pause, made them uncertain.

Rose came within inches of the fox, who bared his teeth, lowered his head, and refused to give ground. He lunged at her, and she backed up, growling slowly, steadily, and then she moved off to the right of the fox, making him turn, as she circled around behind him in a sudden herding move, lunging forward, nipping at his tail and haunches. She saw in his eyes that he had lost a measure of his calm. He'd never seen this sort of movement before. He had been expecting a charge, a fight.

The fox lunged and nipped at her shoulder, but got only fur, and Rose lowered her head and tore at his throat, drawing blood and a sharp yelp. Then she jumped back and circled again, moving sideways, staring at the fox, confusing him further.

The fox was clever, had chosen his approach well. He could not have guessed that Rose would come in from the far side. The wild dog could see the fox, but he could not get at him, even though he made a fearful amount of noise.

The fox listened to the roaring, and turned as Winston pecked at his tail from the rear. Rose growled and lowered her head to charge again.

The fox backed up, looked around, calculated. Rose sensed that he was much like her, that he moved in the same deliberate ways.

This barn was different from his usual hunts, a solitary stalking of rabbit, cat, or mouse. This challenger—this dog—was a strange animal, and she behaved erratically, and seemed determined. Rose waited. There was no need to fight. She could almost see the fox make up its mind. Finally, slowly, deliberately, the fox turned, darted up onto a hay bale, then out through the broken window and into the dark.

Winston huffed and clucked and the hen ran back to the other side of the coop with the others. The rooster strutted proudly in a circle around the floor of the barn.

The wild dog quieted, and Rose stuck her head out into the night to make sure the fox was really gone, and that there were no others. The tracks were already being covered over with fresh-blown snow, but she could hear him making his way through the drifts and over the fence. She looked at the hen, who had a wound on one of her thighs, which was bleeding slightly. She saw that Winston was not injured, and that she had escaped intact herself.

She jumped back down off the raised platform and onto the barn floor, where the wild dog was lying on the ground, panting. He was exhausted from his efforts to get to the fox. She touched her nose to his and he walked over to the straw and curled up, falling asleep immediately.

Rose made her way back to the farmhouse, through the snow. When she was back inside, she ambled up the stairs to check on Sam. He was still asleep.

Sam had no idea what Rose did at night. When she found something wrong—a predator, a sick sheep, a fence blown open—she barked or growled to awaken him. Otherwise, her night rounds were her own business, her secret.

Sometimes, in the morning, when he got up, he looked at her, and asked, "So, how was the night, girl? Everything quiet?" But he knew that some parts of her life were hers alone, and he would never know about them. That there were things that went on in her world all the time that he would never see or grasp.

On this night, she was watching her world turn white, a wall of wind and snow coming between her windows and the barn animals. She was feeling the storm rage, filling up the world around her. Cold crept in around the window frame, as did some powdery snow blown in by the wind.

Rose sighed, shook herself off, and lay down. Sam was exhausted from his previous day trudging between the barn and pastures, dragging water and hay, checking generators, clearing gates, chipping ice, knocking snow off rooftops, kicking, shoveling, and cursing at the massive storm. His deep sleep revealed that he was stiff and drained.

At night, in the dark, sitting by a window, pictures often came streaming through her mind. When Sam was asleep, and there was no work to do, the sounds of the farm and the world beyond seeped into her consciousness. Ewes breathing. Cows snorting. Cats hunting. Bats flying.

Tonight—wind and snow, wind and snow. She had never witnessed so bleak and foreboding a landscape, and it stirred something in her, and in her memory. In the very darkest hours of the night, she closed her eyes, thought of warmth, of green hills rolling out of sight, of sheep stretched almost to the horizon and grass bent in the wind as far as the eye could see.

Rose opened her eyes. She heard a thump from the rear of the house and rushed to a window at the back. She saw a long chunk of drainpipe blow off the roof and fly out toward the pasture and into the dark. She growled.

Storms had always frightened her, especially thunder and lightning. So did gunshots and sudden noises. They were inexplicable, and she had no sense of how to respond to them. She ran back to check on Sam, who was still asleep.

She sniffed his leg, touched his knee with her nose. She

went into the kitchen, gulped down some water, ate some food, and stuck her head out of the dog door.

Although the snow was already coming up to the ground-floor windows, Sam had built a dormer to shield the back door—and the dog door—from snow and rain. Rose could still open it, but if she went out, she would quickly run into a wall of snow and drifts.

She could hear the sheep calling out to their lambs and to one another, though it was muffled by the storm. She could barely see the barn. In seconds, her nose was covered in snow. She drew her head back inside and lay down. She closed her eyes.

There was a continuous sound now, a roaring of air, and a shifting of snow on the roof, and none of it was especially familiar to her. It was difficult for her to lie still for too long.

Rose thought she heard a movement outside and ran to the window again, but this time saw only some snow sliding off the barn roof, slowly, hitting the ground with a thud.

She moved around upstairs, from window to window, looking out, seeing little, hearing the wind, watching the snow, feeling the cold. She listened for further sounds from the barns and the pastures, but she heard nothing, not even the complaining of the goats.

Sam moved in his sleep, rolled over. She hopped up on his bed, sniffed his hand, and he mumbled something to her. She returned to the window.

The storm made her even more alert, hypersensitive to sound and movement. She did not panic, but she was keenly tuned to danger, and a sense of that suffused her being—her body, which was tense, even rigid, and her mind, which was spinning. A storm outside, a storm inside.

* * *

A<small>T LONG LAST</small> day came, although not the sun. The storm was blowing harder than ever, the farmhouse groaning in the wind and thick new snow still falling.

Sam came downstairs, made coffee, and then stood for a long time looking out the windows. He told Rose they would stay inside, but he lasted only a few minutes before pulling on his boots and reaching for his heavy gloves and hooded jacket.

Rose rushed out the door ahead of him, watching him for instructions and commands, surveying the farm and the animals.

He threw hay to the cows, hauled some on a sled out to the sheep. Every movement was difficult in this snow. He chipped at the ice in the troughs where the deicers had either broken or simply could not keep up.

Then he called Rose back to the house with him. She was so encrusted in snow she looked like an all-white dog. He shook off his own coat before taking it off.

He told Rose to stay while he sat at the kitchen table, both of them anxious but unable to do more. He said neither of them should go out in the storm right now, that they would be in for the day if it kept up like this.

Rose edged toward the back door several times, and each time he called her back, the last time a bit sharply. No more work today.

With no work to do, Rose drifted. She went from room to room, window to window. In the bedroom, Rose found a trunk, and when she put her nose to it she smelled Katie, whined, and wagged her tail. Rose was a quiet dog, barking sometimes when working, rarely whining. Once in a great while, she howled at the full moon, or at the sound of a siren on a distant road. Otherwise, she rarely made much noise.

She went downstairs, drank some more water, ate some more food. It was difficult to be still; when she was moving, her senses took over, and drowned out the pictures in her head.

She lay down outside Sam's room.

An hour later, Sam could be still no longer and was back outside, Rose alongside, trying to help the animals, attempting to keep the delicate inner workings of the farm going.

FARMERS KNOW as well as anyone how nature works. You could plan and plant and hammer and nail, and run a good farm, Sam would often tell Katie, and there would be a flood or a drought or a storm, and all of your work, your whole livelihood, would be right there on the line.

He had never conceived of a storm like this, though.

Nor had he imagined being alone in this, without Katie. He had lost not only her but the family they had hoped to have, and he didn't know if he would ever have these things again.

At these moments, he would sometimes look at Rose, who was always watching him, watching the farm, ready for anything, and he thanked God that he had her. He'd thought at first that he was getting just a dog. Now he understood only too well that she had become something else, something more. He did not even want to think of being on this farm alone without Rose.

Like all farmers, he kept going. You did what you could, until you couldn't do any more, and fate took over. You didn't worry about it or complain about it. Sam didn't quit, and neither did Rose.

He brought out buckets of warm water and hauled them to the troughs. He started up the tractor again and briefly tried to move snow to make paths, so he could haul hay. This time he saw that the drifts reached his waist. He covered the tractor with the tarpaulin.

He had only one other idea for the frozen troughs. He brought out the Salamander heating unit most farmers used in the winter to thaw out engines and frozen machines. It worked like a small jet engine: A powerful diesel-powered heating unit blew fire through a three-foot tube. Sam pulled the cord and a flame shot out, melting some of the ice and snow. But the minute he turned it off, the unit froze again, and he had little fuel to keep it going. He abandoned the troughs. He could not keep up, and soon he could barely even stand up. The drifts, the wind, and the savage cold made the footing treacherous, left him numb, soaked, then shivering with cold. It was frostbite weather. Not, he saw, a time for man or beast. Time to get the hell inside.

He had hauled out as much hay as he could, and it was already covered in snow and ice. His shoveling was pointless. His machines had been quickly overwhelmed. He could not keep up.

He retreated inside again, called Rose, and again told her to stay. It was early afternoon now, but it felt like they'd been shuttling back and forth between barns, pastures, and farmhouse for days. Outside was a true whiteout, and he was losing track not only of time, but of where he was.

Sam knew this was dangerous, physically and mentally. He was alone there, he had to remember that. Being alone in a storm like this on a remote farm, even with Rose, you have to take care of yourself, keep focused. Time blurred, the difference between day and night could get lost, and the silence overwhelming.

He resolved once and for all to stay in, and to keep Rose inside as well.

IT WAS CURIOUS, Sam thought, what happened next. He walked into the living room, put wood in the woodstove, returned to the kitchen, turned on the radio, and made himself a cup of tea—Katie had loved tea, but he almost never made any himself and was often confused by all the choices and colors of the packets. He picked a yellow one, put it into his mug, turned on the electric stove, and waited until the water boiled.

He looked at the clock and tried his cell, but it wasn't getting a signal. He picked up the phone, but the line was dead. Soon enough the power would be gone, too, by the sound of the wind. He was certain that many trees would not survive the storm.

Rose sat in the hallway, by the back door, watching him intently, as usual, waiting to see whether there was a chance he was going out to do work. She looked at his feet and saw the thick wool socks, which meant he would be inside. She eyed his soggy parka hanging on a hook, then watched as he made his tea. Sam noticed Rose looking at him curiously, and he realized that she rarely, if ever, saw him by the teapot on the stove. That had been Katie's territory.

He returned her gaze, and he saw her tail twitch. She looked uneasy, he thought.

"You miss Katie, don't you, Rose? Me too."

At the mention of Katie, Rose stirred. She ran to the living room, and looked around, and then loped over to the front door. When she came back, she looked alert and expectant.

Sam reminded himself to stop using Katie's name. It just sent Rose looking for her. And it just left her disappointed.

Sam took his tea out into the living room. As in many old farmhouses, where little time was spent inside, this room was sparsely and inexpensively furnished.

Farmhouses were always getting tracked up with mud, water, or worse. Few farmers had the money or inclination to decorate. What money they had went outside, into the pastures, barns, machinery, and animals.

Katie had meant to get rid of the old orange floral wallpaper, but hadn't gotten to it before she got sick, though she did manage to get the stained acoustic-tile ceiling torn down and painted the rough plaster a soft white. She'd had plans for the rest of the house, but after she died Sam lost all interest in improvement.

The living room, as in most farmhouses, had three sofas, the big green one directly across from the fireplace, the others flanking it, the wing chairs and tables in between. In the winter, living rooms were important, a place for the family to gather and keep warm. This was where Sam and Katie had spent their evenings. The green sofa and two overstuffed wing chairs had belonged to Sam's grandparents, as did the brass poker set in front of the beautiful green-and-blue slate fireplace. The room was lit by two floor lamps, and two kerosene-style table lamps, one with green glass, one red. The room was warm, even intimate and comfortable, if a bit frayed. Three empty vases sat on two mahogany side tables bought by Sam's parents.

The big sofa in front of the fireplace, where Sam and Katie always relaxed in the winter, was the warmest spot in the house, especially when the fireplace was going. In the alcove between the living room and the kitchen was a woodstove, good for the coldest nights, and easier to get going than the fireplace. It could take the sting out of that big, drafty room in ten minutes.

There were two new oil paintings of barns and pastures above the sofas—also Katie's work—and three framed awards from the county recognizing the cleanliness and good management of Granville Farm. One cited Sam's father as Farmer of the Year, 1964, and the other cited Sam in 1992.

On the mantel were three photographs: Sam's grandparents (the picture cracking and yellowed), his parents (a little faded), and a newer crisp digital one of Sam and Katie getting married at the Presbyterian church in town.

Next to it was a single photograph of Rose circling behind the sheep in the main pasture. Sam loved that picture. It was the only one he had of Rose, who would never sit still to pose. She seemed to dislike the camera, always turning her head away from the lens.

A red-and-black square carpet softened the room and muffled the noise of the scratched oak floor. Rose sat by the fireplace in the winter, and when that got too warm, she would move over to the dog bed near the woodstove. Otherwise, she liked to crawl under the blue upholstered chair, which offered just enough space for her to peer out at the room, but hide herself, except for her nose. From there, she monitored the house, scrambling out if Sam headed for the back door or pulled on his boots or jacket.

Sam stirred the fire, then sat down and closed his eyes with a sigh. Every joint in his body was on fire, his knees ached, his toes were still numb from the cold. He listened to the roar of the wind and the sound of the snow hitting the windows, sliding off the roof. He called Rose into the room, and she trotted in and settled down, her eyes fixed on him.

Sam forgot himself now and then. It was, after all, only natural to reach out to pet a good dog.

"This storm is bad. It's going to really hurt us," he said. "Sometimes I wish you could talk."

Although the snow raged outside, it was warm, even cozy in the room. The table lamp by the sofa cast a reddish glow over the room. Sam felt some peace for the first time in days, and he expected he might not feel it again for some time.

"When this is over, I'll get you one of those Frisbees," he said. "Maybe some more treats. We'll have some more fun." He smiled at Rose, and at himself. Fat chance, he thought, of seeing Rose chase a Frisbee. For her, work was the only fun.

She was still watching him, her head cocked, her tail thumping softly on the wooden floor.

He gave up trying to touch her—there wasn't going to be any cuddling on the sofa—and watched as her bright eyes locked onto his. He smiled at her, reached into his pocket, and tossed her a soggy biscuit that had been there a while. She stared at it as if it were a rock, and he shook his head.

"What kind of dog are you, anyway?" he asked softly, and then closed his eyes to go to sleep.

Rose was confused by Sam. He was standing where Katie used to stand, pouring water into a cup that Katie often used. She recognized Katie's name when he spoke it, and she set off to find her, to find her anywhere. She was puzzled that Sam would be speaking her name and yet she could not find her. On Rose's map, most things stood out sharp and clear. Katie did not.

Then he moved to the sofa in front of the fire and called her to him. He spoke to her, but there were no commands that she recognized and few words she knew. His voice was soft, and she recognized the affection in it. He kept looking out the window, at the snow, and Rose sensed he was speaking to her about it, trying to communicate something.

She was distracted. The wind was breaking off limbs all over the woods and pastures, and snow was falling off barns, trees, and the roof of the farmhouse. The wind, to her, was nearly deafening, and sometimes seemed as if it would swallow the farm whole.

Rose was unnerved by the snow sliding off the roof, even though Sam couldn't hear it in the wind. She was very aware of the storm's power. It was different, and she sensed its menace, and the responses of all of the animals. It was a dangerous thing.

She heard the sheep speaking softly among themselves, the cows grunting and calling out to one another, the chickens clucking softly in their sleep, Carol snorting as she nosed through the snow in search of hay. She heard the coyotes out in the woods, in the middle of the storm, hunting. Of all the sounds, the snow falling frightened her the most, and she wanted to go upstairs and crawl under Sam's bed, where she went during thunderstorms. But she couldn't leave him.

She studied Sam intently, turning her nose to him, smelling the sadness and the sorrow, the grief that had welled up inside him for some time and was now an everyday part of him.

He reached his hand out to her, and she instinctively backed away. She did not like to be touched, and Sam almost never tried. Katie had been different. She used to stroke Rose's head and back, which Rose had come to like after a while.

She knew Sam was talking about her, but she did not understand why now, in this place and time, though she could read the appreciation in his voice, see it in his eyes, the way he held his body. She sensed a need in him, but not one she could fill.

It evoked something powerful in her, connected them. She laid her ears back gently, wagged her tail almost imperceptibly, all the emotion she could show. She sat there watching as he drifted into sleep, and she listened to the soft snoring and the occasional moan.

Rose drew closer, watching his body move as he breathed, shifted, and stirred. She listened to his heartbeat, the fluids in his stomach, heard the blood flowing through his veins. She sensed his dreams, even if she could not see or understand them. She knew every part of him.

After a moment, she moved slowly forward and rested her head in his hand, which lay outstretched on the edge of the sofa.

She closed her eyes, and remained there while he slept, listening to the stories the wind was carrying.

THE AFTERNOON became dreamlike. Rose, not accustomed to inactivity, fell into a gauzy kind of state inside the farmhouse. She closed her eyes, rested, and dreamed, alongside Sam.

When images filled her sleeping mind, they usually came from her life: Sam, Katie, the farm. But sometimes—these were rare—they came from somewhere else, from her deepest sleep, or from great fatigue. Sometimes even from fear.

She would close her eyes and drift, and as the long, strange day wore on, the images changed, went deeper, farther.

The woodstove was roaring, and outside the wind was howling steadily; she had by now nearly grown used to the rhythmic, almost hypnotic sounds of snow being whipped against the windowpanes.

It was almost as if she were telling herself a story. She went farther and farther back, her mind a movie reel moving so rapidly it was a blur. Everything looked different, smelled different. Houses, roads, machines vanished, and there was only the rich, primal smell of woods, grass, death, and blood. The air was especially rich in smells, and the light was clear, almost blinding, and the dark was blacker than any night Rose had ever seen, the stars so much brighter and closer.

In her story, Rose was small, a puppy, living in the shadow of her mother, her world bounded by a tiny den clawed out of mud and rocks. Then she was suddenly awakened by roars, growls, the sounds of a struggle. She was thrown into the woods, and saw flashes of a large animal—the image isn't clear—appearing, and her mother picked up and dragged off, snarling, fighting, Rose, lying still, paralyzed with confusion and fear. When she woke again she saw the bodies of her brothers and sisters strewn about her, and felt hunger in her belly.

She lay still, absolutely quiet, and when the hunger was too great to bear, she got up and hobbled on her small legs out of the hiding place and into a meadow. There, when she lifted her nose, looking for her mother, she could find no trace of her.

She picked a new scent, one that transfixed her, and began moving toward it through the meadow grass, hearing the ants and bugs and rats and bigger animals moving all around her. She was quiet, freezing at the slightest sound, waiting patiently, as she had been taught.

Despite her hunger and confusion, she was also enchanted. There were so many times she had to hide, from hawks, birds, foxes, wolves, cats, but she seemed to know when to hide and when to move.

She was ravenous now, and losing her caution. Late on the second day she came to the edge of a clearing, where she was amazed to see bright-yellow flames flaring up and down just ahead of her. She had missed the warmth of her mother, but this was a different kind of warmth, and she could feel it from her hiding place in the bushes.

She saw strange creatures—people—for the first time. Some large, and a smaller one. She was intuitively afraid of these creatures, so unlike any she had ever seen, so unlike her mother or brothers and sisters.

They were sitting around the yellow warmth, and at the center of this warmth was a crackling sound and the smell she had caught on the wind, an unbearably good smell that caused her to drool with hunger. This was the scent she had followed through the woods and the meadows.

She edged forward, drawn by the smell. The creatures turned to look at her and two of them stood up, but the smaller one made a sound, and they sat back down, but still looked at her curiously.

After a time the smaller one took something from the warm fire and tossed it to her, making noises that were soft, not dangerous. The food landed a few feet in front of her, and, frightened at first, she jumped back into the tall grass. But this was what she had smelled and had been seeking.

Her hunger battled her fear, her instincts. She took it in her mouth. This was nothing like her mother's milk, and the taste and the smell electrified her.

The people were quiet now, watching her, except for the small one, the girl who tossed another piece of meat out to the edge of the grass. Rose darted out, grabbed it, then ran into the woods, eating it hungrily.

In her story, Rose slept and hid in the woods, dug a hole for herself, stayed quiet. Yet she ventured to the edge of the grass each morning as the people came and went. The little girl approached slowly again, throwing her some meat before leaving again.

For several days they repeated this ritual, the girl coming closer, bringing food, tossing it out, all the while calling to her, speaking soothingly, warmly.

On the third night, the girl came to the edge of the grass and sat down, holding a piece of food. She made warm, strange guttural sounds. She seemed safe to Rose, and so did this place, this cave in the side of a hill, this warmth, this food.

Rose now spent almost all day and night watching the people, waiting for the girl to bring her food. The girl came closer each time, sometimes playing right in front of Rose, tossing sticks in the air. The people pointed and laughed and threw scraps of food.

On this one night, the girl held some food in her hand, and did not throw it onto the grass or into the woods. Rose edged forward. She crept gamely toward the food—slowly, carefully—until she was eating the piece of meat out of the girl's hand. She licked the girl's hand, and the girl, speaking softly, stroked Rose's back and neck. Rose put her head in the girl's hand, and whined softly.

The next day, the girl brought another piece of meat and Rose ate from one end, while the girl held the other. Rose looked forward to her coming, wagged her tail, enjoyed the attention. The girl threw sticks for her, made soothing sounds.

The girl led Rose back to the other people, who also fed

her and spoke in soothing ways to her. That night, she slept just outside the mouth of the cave. And again the next night, and the one after that.

One night, she heard animals approaching outside and she growled and barked, and the people praised her, gave her food, patted her. She then barked whenever she heard a strange noise, or when an animal came near. It became her job to protect them.

She began to focus on what pleased the new creatures in her life, what made them talk to her approvingly, leave extra meat for her. Sometimes she would smell or sense other dogs but did not go out to join them. Instead, she would growl if they approached, and stand between them and the little girl.

She went with the people as they looked for food, when they swam, she lay by them as they ate and slept. There was no reason to wander, because she had food. She was part of a pack again. She had shelter from the rain and heat and cold. She had attention and affection.

One day the people gathered their things and began to leave the place, and the girl called to her. Rose had a choice, to stay or to go with her, and she paused and looked at her home, and then at the girl, and she went with her. It was the biggest choice she had made.

And this is where her story stopped.

ROSE AWOKE FROM her reverie with a start. Sam was gone, but she heard him breathing upstairs. He was in bed. It was unusual for her to sleep while he moved. Her legs ached from trudging through the heavy snow, and the chill seemed to have rooted deeply in her bones. Her paws were swollen and painful, shredded by the ice, and her fur was matted and full of knots.

While Rose slept, night had come again. The wind still howled, and Sam had gone up to bed while she was dreaming. Although she watched from inside the farmhouse, it seemed the storm was hers. She wandered over to the front door, which was covered in drifts and ice, then to the rear door. She could still get outside, but only just. The pasture gates were covered, too. The hay in the feeders was buried, and the water troughs were black and hard.

A little while earlier, the animals had been free to move about their pastures, to the feeders and troughs. Now snow and ice made almost everything impassable. The geography of the farm, the map, had changed. The cows were trapped in the back pasture, the chickens barricaded in the barn, the goats unable to crawl or climb out of their pen, already hungry, although Sam had stuffed every inch of their feeders with hay.

Rose felt compelled to leave the house. She pushed open the small swinging flap, nearly overwhelmed by the ice and heavy snow.

Just outside the door, she scrambled up to the hard windswept surface, now crusted with ice. She slipped and slid to the pasture gate, and began to tunnel to the other side.

EIGHT

ONCE OUTSIDE, ROSE WAS DISORIENTED BY THE STORM'S ferocity. The air was colder than she had ever experienced, and she could not comprehend it. The brutal wind and intense snowfall confronted her with an alien landscape— huge drifts in some places, only a foot or two in others.

Although the snow had drifted over much of the opening in the barn door, there was still room for Rose to wiggle through. Inside, the chickens were in their roosts, and the wild dog—who lifted his head briefly when she came in—was lying on a bale of straw.

The lamb and mother—the pair she and Sam had saved the night before the storm broke—were talking to each other. They were the only two sheep in the big barn. Sam had left the others up in the three-sided pole barn, which was newer and stronger. They couldn't all fit in this building, which, although bigger, was crammed with equipment, and suffered wobbly foundations and a tottering roof.

The scene in the barn seemed natural, but then she caught another scent and heard another cry. This was different, a call of alarm from a mother, calls from the other sheep. The fur on her back stood up, and she heard herself growling, heard the wild dog struggling to his feet. The chickens and rooster were startled awake, and Rose was up over the drift and out the door in a flash. She opened a hole wide enough for the wild dog to follow, and he clambered up behind her.

Nothing about the farm looked the same as it had when she had last been outside.

She could barely see through the snow blowing in her face, and she struggled to get footing on the layer of ice that had crusted over the snow. She felt the sting of the cold in her eyes, in her paws, as the awful night engulfed her, covering her in clumps of ice that clung to her fur, weighing her down.

She heard the wild dog scrambling behind her, trying to keep up, slipping and falling. At first she waited for him, then understood she had to move quickly. She pawed her way through the snow and up the hill toward the run-in pole barn.

Normally, the pregnant ewes would have been in the lambing pens, but Sam had released them so they could find the protection of the pole barn and not be trapped in the exposed pens by the snow or crammed into the big barn, where there was no room for them.

Rose could feel the presence of the frightened ewe up ahead of her, and she could clearly hear the calls of the other sheep, panicked now. They were frantically moving back and forth within their shelter, but Rose's view was blocked by the mounting snow. Running a hundred feet long and twenty feet deep, the pole barn was built so that its back faced the oncoming winds, its strong oak beams sharply slanted to handle the heavy winter snows.

She heard the wild dog barking far behind her now. She made her way up the hill, laboring toward the pole barn, and then, struggling for breath, she pushed her way through the snow and saw the sheep, all jammed into one corner where it was dry and sheltered from the fierce wind.

Rose saw that they were paralyzed with fear, as sheep are when trapped. Off to the right, in the opposite corner of the pole barn, was the ewe, afterbirth trailing from her rear, its smell still fresh, even through the wind and snow.

The mother was in a panic. She ran here and there, calling out for her lamb—a particular kind of call mothers use to locate their offspring. She charged into the snow but was blocked and fell back.

Rose recognized this ewe instantly, one of the oldest and most pliant on the farm. She often retreated into the center of the flock when Rose appeared, wanting no trouble with the dog. But she was also a fiercely protective mother who would lower her head and rush in front of her babies whenever Rose came too close.

When she saw Rose emerge from the blizzard, she did not back off, as she normally would have, or lower her head, but looked at Rose in a way Rose had never seen before—as if pleading. She looked the dog in the eyes, but it was not a challenge, and not just an expression of desperation.

Rose understood sheep better than she understood people, even Sam. Sam often confused her, but the sheep never did.

The ewe was worried about her baby.

Rose stopped in the front of the pole barn, close to the ewe. She caught her breath, shook the snow and ice out of her eyes, leaned down and pulled chunks of ice off of her paws and forelegs with her teeth. Then she raised her nose high in the air. Smells poured through her mind.

The scent of coyotes came to her clearly. She now understood, and plowed forward through the snow, over the ice, into the wind, and off to the right, to where the ewe was looking frantically. It took her what seemed like a long time to get that very short distance, as she kept falling into the drifts through the ice crust, her breath labored from the strain and weight of the snow in her fur. She heard a scratching and wheezing sound and was surprised to see the wild dog coming through the forbidding night close behind her.

After a few minutes, panting harder, her tongue long, Rose made it around the corner of the pole barn to a mound of snow where she could see up the hill. She smelled lamb and she smelled coyote but, at first, could see neither. She heard the shrieking of the wind, the piercing calls of the ewe, the anxious responses of the other sheep.

Rose did know fear, but it was fear of failing, not of other animals, or of injury or death. She'd felt something strange and new when the ewe had turned to her. It was not an image she could recall, but she felt it strongly, not in her nose or in her mind, but deep within her chest. Rose sensed the ewe's emotion and it drove her up the hill. Most of all, she knew it was her job to protect the sheep and lambs.

As she moved a few feet up the hill, she smelled the blood. Some of the drops were still visible in the snow, the scent different from any other.

Blood was familiar to her—she almost always smelled it running through the woods. But Rose had only smelled the blood of a lamb once, when one was born twisted, near death, and Sam had gone to get the rifle and had shot it.

The experience had affected her, left her confused and lethargic for hours, so much so that Sam gave her a day off to get over it. But she remembered it, and knew it now.

She froze. There, not more than a few steps in front of her, was the coyote, the leader, the one she had known as a pup. His eyes were ablaze, and a dead lamb was hanging by the throat from his mouth. Three other coyotes stood in a half circle right behind him. The lamb's head hung off to one side, its eyes closed, its still-warm body hanging down to the ground.

Rose paused to take in this scene, moving in and out of shadow, framed by snow, ice, wind, dark. It was almost like one of her dreams, but her nose told her it was very real.

She was still, but teeming inside. It was not in her work— her map—although there were scenes like it in her memory. It had happened. But it had never happened to her, not in this way.

The coyote's look was plain—he would stand here with the lamb, fight to the death for it, bring it back to his den for his pack, to feed them, save them, get them through the night. In the killing cold, in the mounting storm, his own instincts were as clear as hers: get to food, get to shelter. Quickly. Fresh food was life-and-death to him and his pack.

The lamb had been born quietly, and Rose had not heard or smelled it through the wind and snow. But the coyotes, up-wind of the barn, had been waiting and watching. The leader would have slipped in around the edge of the pole barn, sending the sheep—all but the mother—back into the corner as he grabbed the lamb by the neck. He must have killed it swiftly and taken it up the hill. The carcass, too heavy for him to carry all the way back, he would have meant to dismember there, and he and the other coyotes would bring its parts back through the storm, through the woods, to their den.

The wild dog rounded the pole barn corner and growled. Covered in ice and snow, his fur up, he began to charge up the hill toward the coyote.

* * *

ALL KINDS of pictures flashed through Rose's mind.

One was of her fighting the coyote, trying to drive it off, returning the lamb to the flock. But the lamb was dead. The coyote would fight. The other coyotes would join in. They would not run and leave a fresh lamb in the snow, not now.

Another image was of charging up the hill with the wild dog. This image became clear, the two dogs challenging the coyotes, then it stopped. The wild dog was determined, but not strong enough. She saw him dead.

Rose pictured Sam giving commands. But he faded from her mind. He was not there. Rose's mind flashed backward to some of the other animals she had seen die—sheep of old age, or in childbirth, cows of illness or injury. Those deaths, she recalled, had occurred beyond her ability to react. They were not her responsibility.

A different feeling, a sense of choice, came to her now. She reacted to it.

She showed her teeth, not to the coyote but to the wild dog. Surprised, he stopped. She started down the hill, backing him down, growling, challenging him with her eyes, pushing into him with her head and shoulders, watching his eyes watch the coyote.

She could see without seeing that the coyote was not fighting, was making his way up the hill with the body of the lamb, watching them as he backed away.

Rose could see that the wild dog did not understand what Rose was doing, or why she was reacting to him in this way, but he grasped what she wanted him to do. He was a working dog; he was prepared to fight. But he deferred to her. She knew that he could not challenge her notions of work. He had made decisions, too—many times—but this was hers.

Rose turned and looked back. She saw the trail of blood, a

deep red staining the snow. A moment later, the coyotes and lamb were swallowed up by the storm and the darkness.

She headed back down the hill, the wild dog ahead of her, both tired, struggling to find their footing, to lick their stinging, bloodied paws. They were greeted by the ewe, who wasn't retreating into the corner of the pole barn but coming out with a pleading, expectant look in her eyes.

ROSE TILTED her head, pricked her ears forward, raised her nose in the air, looking for new signs, new signals. But she was getting the same message from everywhere: cold and fear. And the overwhelming backdrop of the monstrous storm.

She was close to the pole barn. The wild dog had gone back inside the big barn. The goats were quiet now. She wondered where Carol, the donkey, was, could not sense or hear her. There was almost too much to keep track of.

The temperature had plunged to far below zero, and the wind howled and seemed to suck the warmth, even the life, out of the farm. It would be dangerous to stop too long in this cold. She felt it in her paws, in her eyes and ears. In such weather animals that did not move or get out of the wind could die easily—frozen to the ground.

Rose looked to the woods, sensed the panic through the trees and the snow and the brush. There were surely animals dying, a few carcasses already lying out in the woods, creatures stricken by exposure to the cold and wind, by exhaustion, weakened by hunger. Perhaps the coyotes would feed on them and stay away.

This kind of cold almost made it painful to breathe. It was draining her as well as the other animals. The cold was coming up from the ground and into her body, through her mouth, eyes and ears. She couldn't bring herself to go back into the shelter of the farmhouse. And Sam did not seem to be coming out for now. She had seen his weariness.

She sensed her limits. Rose could not help Sam deal with the cold—that was in the other realm, the human realm of things, pipes frozen and cracked, machines, stoves, and heaters failing—but the sheep were her job, not Sam's.

The sheep, as attuned to working dogs as the dogs are to them, seemed to sense that Rose was lost, that her world had been turned upside down. They were talking to one another, trying to soothe and be soothed, fighting off panic. In their own suffering and distraction, they had disconnected from her. Weakened and sensing danger, losing energy, terrified of the coyotes, the sheep were clinging to the warmth of one another and huddling together.

Rose made her way into the pole barn, closing her eyes against the ice, the wind flattening her ears, and stood in front of the sheep. The sheep were startled when she reappeared out of the snow and cold not five feet from where they lay. Her eyes told the sheep not to move. They didn't.

Rose shivered in the cold, and her paws ached from the sting of it. Her eyelids were nearly frosted over, but she shook her head and her eyes swept the barn. Two or three of the sheep got up, almost as if out of respect. The others seemed beyond caring.

Rose invoked their ancient relationship. Her presence said, Trust me. Nothing else. We will do what we can. She stared at the sheep so that there could be no mistaking her message.

The Blackface got up, and, one by one, the rest of the ewes and rams followed, meeting her gaze. The sheep stood face-to-face with Rose, and the scene on that snow-swept hill seemed to transform itself into other hills, other storms, other places, this deepest of relationships asserting itself.

The sheep calmed, settled, and began to lie down again.

Rose could not guarantee anything, not food, water, safety, or survival. But she was determined that they would respect her, honor their long history together, and, if it were their time, they would face it together. The story would not end in panic and disconnection, confusion and death. It would end with her trying to lead them, keep them safe.

As the sheep settled, Rose moved deeper into a corner of the barn to get out of the fierce wind. She came face-to-face with a ewe and her newborn lamb, which was shivering in the cold. The milk of the hungry, cold, tired mother was surely weak.

Rose, exhausted but alert, approached the mother, and sniffed the lamb. The baby, not yet knowing the ways of sheep and dogs, stumbled over to Rose and touched her nose against the dog's.

Behind them, the snow obscured the world below.

The lamb crawled next to its mother for warmth, and the ewe nuzzled her baby. Rose turned and began the cold, wet walk back to the barn.

ROSE WAS EXHAUSTED, not only physically but in a new and different way. She was used to being tired but not to being so drained, challenged by so many unfamiliar and disturbing situations. And she was not yet done.

A dull-gray morning was beginning to break. It was the third day of thick and swirling snow. Rose stopped and surveyed the strange scene, adjusted her map, but failed to keep it clear. Down below, and to the right, the farmhouse sat in the dark, the back nearly buried in snow. It was as if Sam were trapped inside now.

Nearby, the big barn, with the chickens and the strutting, pompous rooster. Next to it, the goat pen—the jeering, raucous creatures' usual complaints softer now, muffled by the storm. One of the lambs, briefly added to the map, was now gone, the other bleating softly. Farther to the left, Brownie the steer and some of the cows stared up at her anxiously.

Rose was confused. Sam was integral to her work, but at this moment she was on her own. And it seemed that all of the animals—the stricken mother, the wild dog, the other sheep, the steers and cows, even the loud and obnoxious goats—were looking to her.

Her cherished map was in shambles—it was changing too rapidly. The storm was bigger than anything in her experience. Rose felt a sense of awe and wonder, a great stirring inside her mind. Her life and work had always been directed before, comprehensible, part of her experience, shaped by her instincts, by Sam, by the predictable routines, rhythms, and seasons of the farm. It seemed that her world was falling to pieces, like little drops of blood scattered across the snow.

SAM WATCHED ROSE as she worked her way back behind the farmhouse, the pathway nearly impassable. She got to the dog door, protected by the overhang, and dragged herself through the kitchen. Sam was now awake and dressed, sitting on the couch drinking coffee, and looking anxiously at the white outside the windows. He seemed paralyzed as the blizzard enveloped his whole life, everything he had worked for.

But yesterday afternoon's inactivity was a momentary

pause in the battle; it would not be repeated. He had to keep trying, to fight to save what he could—every water pipe, gate, and animal.

THE POWER WENT OUT as Sam walked toward the back of the house. The lamps flickered two or three times—the fur on Rose's ruff went up at the shifting light—and then went black. After a moment of darkness, a bulb in the living room flickered on again.

"The emergency generator," said Sam, "it kicks on automatically." But it was diesel-powered and would last only a day or two, and it powered only a few lights downstairs plus the kitchen stove. Everything else—the power to most of the house, the barns, the well pump, the heating system—was shut down. It was better than nothing, but this was one more hard blow.

"I'm surprised it took this long," he told Rose, "when you consider the wind."

He was putting his coat on, looking for dry gloves, pulling up his boots. "I can't just stay in here," he said. "Let's go check the snow on the barn roof. It must be getting bad. Maybe I can get a ladder up there."

Rose did not understand these words, and Sam did not sound like he usually did when giving her commands. But still, she grasped the call to work.

She followed as he clambered out the back door, bowed his head low in the wind to keep the snow out of his face as he headed for the barn, Rose following close behind him.

* * *

SAM SLID OPEN the barn door and clambered up to the rack where the few remaining hay bales were stored. He took out a long cord and tied one bale to his belt, and then heaved it onto his back. Then he turned and waded out into the storm, up the hill, to the goat pen. The frightened goats were huddled in one of their sheds and Sam took off his gloves, grabbed his knife, and cut the hay bale, stuffing it into the shed. He went back into the barn and repeated the process, hauling enough hay into the goat shed and the adjoining feeder to last them at least a couple of days.

"To give 'em a chance," he told Rose.

He'd been talking to her more and more in the last day or so to fend off his deepening isolation and despair. He found, a bit to his surprise, that talking to Rose, sharing his plan with her, was soothing. And although he knew she didn't understand most of his words, she seemed to accept it as part of her job now to listen to him.

"This storm is awful," he said. "Things will really start to get bad if it goes on like this. I hate to sit in the house and watch all of my animals freeze and die. But it's almost impossible to move now."

It was difficult to speak over the wind, and yet he didn't feel as if he were talking to himself. Rose was much more a presence than he ever thought a dog could be. But still, he was struggling to keep even. He wondered if he was beginning to lose his mind. Rose was so steady, she made a difference, he kept telling himself. She did.

"Rose," he said. "I miss Katie every day, but I'm glad she didn't see this. This would have been awful for her."

Sam knew there was not enough hay for all the animals for very long—he had been expecting another shipment when the storm broke. He had converted his hay pastures to more prof-itable crops—corn, potatoes—and bartered for hay with some other farmers.

The animals would eat it all at once, not saving any.

There wasn't much point in putting too much out now, anyway, as it would be covered in snow and ice, and inedible. But the goats were hardy. He had given them enough to hold them for a while. He'd do the same for the others.

He put what he could in the sheds, feeders, and pole barn. It wasn't enough, but it was something.

And now he needed to clear the roof.

He pushed open the gate and squeezed through the open-ing in the sliding door, wet snow falling off him, the cats and chickens circling, hoping he was bringing food. "Stay out, Rosie," he said, pulling out an aluminum ladder and a long rake he used to get snow off the slate roofs that covered all of the buildings of the farm. This was a ritual that she knew well, she'd seen him do it often enough. As long as he'd been a farmer, Sam had heard stories of snow collapsing roofs, espe-cially old barn roofs, which were not always strong enough and often were not slanted steeply enough.

Sam felt energized, driven even, at the sight of enormous amounts of snow piling up everywhere. He was worried about everything on the farm, but for the moment he was focused on the rear of the big barn. It had a good slant for normal snow—it would build up, and then slide off. But he had never seen this much, and it was piling up perilously high. Five feet or more had fallen now, and it was much higher in some places from the wind. Rose watched from beside the feeder.

* * *

SAM HAD DRAGGED the ladder outside and to the rear of the barn, using his feet and a shovel to clear a flat space to plant it. Twice the gusting winds blew the ladder out of his hands and off to the side, but Sam braced the bottom with a rock and some cement blocks, packing the bottom rung in snow. When it was solid enough, he began the laborious and slippery climb up the ladder, step by step, scraping the ice off his boots on each successive rung, dragging the long snow rake up by one hand.

It took Sam nearly a half hour to get up to the top rung, battered by cold, snow, and wind each step of the way. Twice the ladder shifted in the wind and he grabbed on to the drainpipe. The rake slipped out of his hand, and he had to retrieve it and begin the climb all over again.

Rose stood looking up at the base of the ladder, waiting for instructions. She could barely see Sam when he got to the top, but then she heard him muttering and grunting as he reached the rake out to try and poke some of the heavy snow off the roof.

"God, I've never seen so much," he shouted down. "Get back, Rosie."

Rose heard Sam's "get to work" voice, shook herself off, and backed up, as the chunks of snow began to come off the roof.

Then her ears and ruff went up as she heard a fearful shout. There was a roar of moving snow, and Sam came hurtling off the ladder top. Rose darted forward as he fell to the snow below, but was forced back as a mountain of white came crashing down, first on top of him, and then on her, too. Everything went black.

NINE

ROSE WAS NEAR THE EDGE OF THE AVALANCHE, STUNNED AND buried under several feet of snow. It cut off her smell and sight, and left her in a kind of void she had never known before. But the bulk of the snow had fallen on Sam, so although she was frightened and confused, she quickly shook herself alert, and clawed her way up and out.

She couldn't see or hear Sam, but she spotted the edge of the ladder sticking out of the snow. A huge mound had fallen off the roof, a wet and heavy blanket. The wild dog came hobbling out of the barn and stood staring at her, confused and alarmed by the noise.

Rose was, for a moment, frozen. She never experienced panic, always stayed focused on her work. Her first instinct was to go find Sam and bring him back here—to where he already was—and she actually started for the house. She was disoriented, her work plan fuzzy. She had lost track of Sam.

Then she paused, remembering that he was not in the house. She looked at the roof, at the ladder, and then at the wild dog. She ran into the barn, where Sam had gotten the ladder, then bolted back outside to the spot where she had last seen Sam, and studied the ladder sticking out of the snow.

She focused all of her senses on the snow, closing her eyes in case she might hear or smell or intuit something by concentrating. The wild dog remained still, his brown and black ruff covered in snow, watching her.

The sheep up in the pole barn called out to her, as if she might take them to pasture, and food, but Rose ignored them. She looked up at the Blackface, and her look was clear: Stay where you are.

Rose turned back to the pile of snow. A mesmerizing rainbow of sounds flashed before her. She heard birds out in the forest, squirrels gnawing on nuts, rabbits burrowing beneath the snow, raccoons tunneling beneath tree roots, mice scampering in the corners of the barn, the barn cats slinking across the barn rafters. She heard the shrieking wind, the groan of the snow on the barn roofs, and on barn roofs miles away, the ticking of the living room clock in the farmhouse, the sound of heavy, wet snow falling.

She took all of this in—the storm, the barns, the animals, the wind, the noises and colors—and then, out of this riotous stream, a cluster of images coalesced in her mind and she locked in on the sounds and feelings close to her. She heard one group of sounds—a groan, a sigh, breathing—a few feet from where the ladder lay, and she zeroed in on the spot.

She began digging frantically. She used both of her front paws, planting her hind legs deep in the snow behind her, using them to keep her steady. Occasionally, she leaned forward and bit out chunks of snow with her teeth. Her front legs became a pinwheel, digging out one bit of snow after another, pumping, clawing, furiously, continuously.

Soon she was panting, her tongue hanging down toward

her feet. Snow and ice flew up into her face, onto her fur. She barely stopped to shake herself off, and only once or twice did she pause to gulp down some snow, having grown overheated and thirsty. Her paws were now bloody, pieces of snow stained red as they flew behind her.

She kept going, digging and digging, the front of her body inclining farther and farther down, almost falling forward into the deepening hole. Fortunately the snow was still soft and gave way to her digging.

The wild dog's senses, she knew, were not as keen, but by watching her he knew the spot she was focusing on, and, without any kind of overt communication, Rose's eyes led him to the left of the protruding ladder.

The wild dog, weaker but still intense, began digging next to her. The snow flew in a steady stream behind the two dogs, forming scattered piles beneath them.

Carol looked over the fence in puzzlement, a donkey's curiosity.

The wind and snow were so intense that the two dogs could barely see each other. After a few minutes, Rose saw that the wild dog's paws were also bleeding, and that he was weakening. With a stare, she backed him off, and he accepted this command and sat down.

Suddenly, Rose barked, once, then twice, then in a continuous rhythm. The wild dog was puzzled by this, as were the other animals. This kind of barking was not at all familiar to them.

It was not meant for them.

BENEATH THE SNOW, Sam was awakening. He was barely conscious but could feel the cold, the damp, the blackness. He remembered only the snow sliding into him and sweeping him off the roof, and the long, black fall onto the snowy ground, and the feeling of being hammered as the snow crashed on top of him. Then he had blacked out, but now he remembered where he was, what had happened. He felt a rush of terror, but stayed calm. Lord, he thought, how deep am I?

His right arm was twisted beneath him, and the pain was excruciating. He could not move an arm or a leg, and, fighting back panic, began to murmur the Twenty-third Psalm to keep his mind from running away. He imagined Rose had been buried, too, and felt a pang for the poor dog if she were trapped beneath the snow like he was.

He struggled, trying to push upward, pressing the snow with his good left arm and then with one of his legs. It didn't move an inch.

There was no one to hear him, or look for him, no way for him to get out. Soon he would freeze.

So this then, he thought, was the end. He remembered his father always telling him never—ever—panic. Farms were full of dangers, he'd said, and panic never helped. Sam thought of Katie, and of the idea of joining her. He thought of Rose, the dutiful creature, who would be looking for him.

Best to be calm and let the cold and darkness do their work.

He couldn't imagine any way of digging himself out of such a mound, or of seeing light again. He felt another surge of fear in his chest and fought against it. He thought of talking to Katie, of the farm, of his parents and brothers. *The Lord is my shepherd. I shall not want.*

"Rose," he whispered. "Rose."

* * *

Up above, it was getting dark, and the farm animals were settling in for the night, both aware of and impervious to the drama unfolding around them. They'd seen the snow fall, watched Rose struggle to get up, saw Sam disappear. But none of it had any meaning for them. In their world, life was now about food and water, and their instinct to survive.

Down below, Rose stopped her digging, lifted her ears. She'd heard something. Her name. Sam's whispered voice. She was tiring, her pace a little slower, but at this she resumed digging even harder than before.

She could see nothing but the hole she was making, and the snowy silhouette of the wild dog, who would get up and dig, and then lie down when it got to be too much. Rose let him set his own pace, but if he dug for too long, she would growl at him or give him a look, and he would back off.

Every few minutes, Rose would bark, then pause to listen, trying to focus and pick the groaning and breathing out of the cacophony of images and smells and sounds that were pouring into her head.

More blood was seeping from her paws now, and they stung sharply. Her limbs were stiff, and she was cold and hungry. But the rest of the world had virtually disappeared from her consciousness, and she saw only the hole in front of her, but was aware of the wild dog, exhausted by now, unable to dig, offering support only by his presence.

Rose had no measure of time. She could not know that this was the evening of the storm's third day. She was aware of the gathering darkness, certainly of the deepening cold, the wind, and mounting snow, and she kept hearing ominous creaks and groans from above her. Every now and then, she looked up to see if any more snow was falling down on them.

* * *

SAM HAD NO NOTION of how long he had been under the snow, how long he had been unconscious. He felt his limbs numbing, and he was grateful he had room to move his head so at least he could breathe. He imagined it was better to die of cold than suffocation.

After a while he imagined he heard a bark, but he could not believe that it was real.

He thought he might be dreaming.

He kept reciting the Twenty-third Psalm, not because he was especially religious but rather because it was the only prayer he knew. He went over the bills, the lists of farm chores, things that needed to be repaired, plans to take the sheep and cows to market, the latest prices. The long list of farm chores was a gift as it occupied his mind, and kept him calm.

Sam was claustrophobic, and he feared falling into that hysteria. The pain in his arm and his side was becoming un-bearable. He had lost feeling in his toes and fingers.

He had heard that freezing to death was one of the more pleasant ways to die, in that you ironically felt warm and just went to sleep. Being buried alive was something else, but he forced his mind elsewhere. What if he could join Katie? What if Rose was there as well? So many people believed it—his par-ents had—that maybe it could be true. Would dogs go to heaven? Would he? Katie had, he knew that. Would there be work for him and Rose to do? He loved his farm, but his life was a struggle. Perhaps . . .

Sam's thoughts were interrupted by a series of ex-cited barks, close now. Something was scratching around his chest.

* * *

Rose sank into a state of absolute focus. She dug and dug and dug, aware neither of pain nor cold, only of Sam beneath the snow.

She now knew precisely where Sam was, heard his breathing, his heartbeat, sensed his resignation. They were together again, only this snow between them. He was alive. Her work had never been clearer, or her purpose so intense in every part of her.

The snow kicked up in steady bursts behind her. She was possessed. The sheep looked down at this eerie scene in wonder and confusion.

Abruptly, Sam felt the wind on his face. He looked up and saw huge flakes of snow blotting the dark sky above. He felt a tongue licking furiously at his face. Rose was whining in excitement, circling, licking and nipping at him.

He raised his head, pushed himself up a bit with his left arm, popping up into the sweet cold air. His face was covered with more licks, and Rose, usually reserved, was squirming in excitement. She nipped him again at his ear.

Whenever Sam fell, Rose always rushed over and nipped at his ear until he got up, and she began nipping now. Get up, get up.

"Hey, girl," he said, struggling to focus and orient himself, then to sit up and crawl out of the snow. Nothing of the visible surroundings made any sense. "Did you dig me out? Are you okay?"

He rolled over onto his left side, and Rose came closer,

licking him now in a more workmanlike manner, clearing the snow and ice off his face.

Sam pulled himself out of the hole, slowly, crying out in pain, while Rose whined and circled him. He felt an odd, painful relief at being back in the open air, even in this awful storm. He couldn't get over what Rose had done—that she had devised and executed a plan to rescue him. It was no easier to believe the enormous pile of snow in a mound behind where she had been digging.

He looked over at the wild dog, lying in the snow, panting, his own old paws bleeding and torn. So he had been digging, too. Sam nodded to him, a kind of thanks.

He looked up to see how the barn was. The gutters were torn off, along with a chunk of slate and wood.

When he tried to move, Sam shouted out in pain. Rose stepped back, focused again. Sam knew he was seriously injured.

And he saw that Rose was hurt as well. He looked down at the blood in the snow, then noticed her paws. He shook his head.

"Thanks, Rose. Thanks. Good girl." Rose's tail was wagging steadily. But it was no time for praise. She still had work to do. The snow was falling thickly, the wind blowing furiously, the cold bitter, relentless, and Sam couldn't move.

Sam could feel his right arm dangling, and his right knee was in so much pain he could barely move. He knew it would be a long crawl back to the farmhouse, that he had no hope of standing or walking, but he also knew he had better get there, get inside, and get help. He would not last much longer outside.

Sam looked at his watch. It was just after eight p.m. He

feared frostbite in his fingers or toes. He figured he had been in the snow for nearly an hour, and Rose, who was hobbling, had probably been digging the whole time. He leaned over and patted her head, and she licked his hand.

He moved slowly, pulling himself through the snow until the pain was too much, then taking a breath. He had to keep going. He had to stop dwelling on the cold. There was a first-aid kit in the bathroom. He thought of the emergency plan the state police had set up for crises, and he knew where the flare gun was in the pantry. According to the plan, watchers would be looking for flares in the morning, at midday, and then again in the evening. He might be past the evening's appointed time. He'd probably have to hold out until morning.

Every farmer knew the plan. More than one had used it— in floods, fires, when tractors fell over, or limbs got caught in hayers, or cows kicked someone in the head.

The flare guns were powerful, bright, and if shot high could be seen for miles, through clouds and snow. It was his only chance. He would fire off one round in the night, just in case, and one in the morning.

But, injured as he was, he wasn't ready to abandon the farm and the animals. Maybe . . . maybe he could get some hay out to the animals one more time before they carried him away.

Outside, Rose followed slowly as Sam crawled, then collapsed, then crawled again, inch by inch making his way back to the farmhouse. He pushed and pulled with his good hand and his feet against the snow. Sam had torn a ligament in his leg in a fall from a tractor years earlier, and he could feel pain coming from that old injury as well as his arm. It was blinding, but he hoped if he kept the pressure off it he would be able to stand up once he got inside, out of the snow and ice. It was impossible to walk through the drifts, but he only had about two hundred feet to go.

By the time he made it to the farmhouse door, he could see the clock in the kitchen through the window. It was nearly nine. Rose followed all the way, sometimes circling ahead, then coming back as if to push from the rear.

"Rose, we have to get each other through this," he said. "If we're lucky, we'll get help in the morning."

He thought Rose looked at him curiously, tilting her head. Lord, he thought, how must I look to her, crabbing around like this? Can she know how hurt I am?

ROSE SNIFFED the blood on the ground, a trail both of them had left from the barn through the snow to the back door, then followed Sam inside.

The light powered by the generator lit the entranceway in the back, the kitchen, and the living room. Sam fumbled in a drawer and then a light appeared in his hand. He lit a thick candle.

Rose waited outside the bathroom where Sam had gone, but when she heard his shouts, she ran in. Sam was leaning into the sink, gripping a towel between his teeth.

"God," he said. Rose's head tilted, and she tensed, her nostrils flaring, as she listened to his cries.

She saw his bent posture. She saw everything. The twisted grimace in his face. The gasps and grunts and shouts of pain. She smelled his injuries, the mangled arm, felt the heat from his arms and legs, the cold from the frostbite.

She had heard some of these noises from him once or twice before, when he had fallen off the tractor and injured his shoulder, and again just after Katie had left the house that last time.

He was talking to her now, looking at her. She understood the hurt, the alarm. Only a few words were clear to her, "hay," and "sheep," and "work," and then, once or twice, her name and Katie's. But Sam was not making any sense, did not sound anything like himself.

Rose could not really differentiate between physical pain and grief. They both sounded the same to her, both generated powerful smells that alarmed her, giving rise to her own anxiousness and fear. She had no idea what to do in response.

ONCE SAM got his coat and shirt off—an agonizing process—he saw that his arm was broken. The bone was poking through the skin below the elbow.

It took him a long time to wrap a gauze bandage over his shattered, bloody arm, fashioning a sling out of a long towel and tying a knot with his teeth. He stayed calm, knowing his life depended on it. He found some adhesive tape, which he unrolled with his teeth and used to help hold the sling in place. He took a half dozen headache tablets, gulping them down with water from his cupped hand. His small generator had kept water running from the well, and there was still some pressure in the tank.

Drops of sweat were forming on his forehead. Rose came over to sniff the fear, and wonder at it. She looked anxious, concerned.

But there was nothing for her to do.

With his good hand, Sam reached for his cell phone, then put it down. It was dead. He was grateful at least that he had bought the generator. He would have some light, at least until morning. And the woodstove was still going and would give him some heat. He could not haul logs to the fireplace.

He was shivering. He knew he was disoriented, probably on the verge of shock, and that he would only get worse.

ROSE HAD NEVER SEEN Sam so ashen. She could smell the wounds, feel the pain, sense the confusion and distress. She whined, agitated and unsure. She turned toward the rear of the house to listen for sounds from the barn or the pasture. She didn't hear any.

She lay down to lick her own wounds, her shredded, bloodstained paw pads. Every step in the snow and ice had sent pain shooting up her legs.

She looked up when Sam dropped to one knee on the bathroom floor, grimacing in pain, and then called her, told her to stay, and shook some powder onto her bloody pads, telling her to be still.

IT TOOK A WHILE for Sam and Rose to make their way back into the living room, near the stove. Sam walked slowly across the floor, opened the stove door with one hand, and threw a log in, then closed the door again. He took a bottle of scotch from the cabinet on the wall and swallowed several mouthfuls, then came over and lay on the couch, his arm wrapped in his improvised sling and held close to his body.

He was still in his wet pants, and shirtless, but he had no energy to do more. He pulled the blanket that lay on the couch over himself. He was half-asleep almost immediately, breathing heavily, mumbling, occasionally crying out when his arm moved or shifted.

Rose padded over to his side, put her nose on his out-stretched hand, which was hanging off the sofa. He reached his hand down, let her lick it.

"Hey, girl," he said. "I'm in trouble here. We have to get out of here, both of us. Maybe . . . when the snow stops . . ."

ROSE LISTENED. Sam's heart was strong, his breathing steady. But she could feel the spreading pain, and sadness. She smelled the blood, sniffed the broken arm, the bone, sensed the shock that Sam was slipping into. Images raced through her mind.

In her head, she moved sheep, cows, watched for coyotes. None of these images helped her, or told her what to do. Help-lessness was alien to her. She whined, sniffed at Sam's frostbit-ten hand.

She decided she would sit by him, watch and wait. She couldn't grasp the idea of help from outside, medicine, or res-cue. Only acceptance of the reality of the moment, of what she could see, and what her instincts conveyed to her. And a search for the work to do.

Rose went to the water bowl, drank half of it, then ate some of the kibble Sam had put out for her. She was limping off her right knee, which was badly sprained, perhaps torn from pushing through the snow. Her paws stung, but the bleeding had stopped. Her legs ached.

The ice had cut and bloodied her nose as well. Now and then she shook her head, trying to shake away the pain. Snow and ice clumps still hung off her tail and coat. She lay down and closed her eyes.

Half asleep, Sam called out to her, "Rose, girl . . . where are you?"

Her ears shot up, and she was by the sofa in an instant. She put her nose to his hand. His eyes were closed, his chest moving in time with his breath.

After Sam fell back asleep, Rose went to sit near the kitchen window. The Sam she knew, the one whose routines and commands defined every day of her life, seemed to have been blown away by the storm, along with the predictable, defined life she had known.

The past couple of days, before he had fallen off the barn roof, he was always going to the window, sometimes rushing outside to drag hay to the feeders, shovel snow from the paths, try to clear the barn doors, bang the frozen deicers with his hammer, haul warm water to the troughs, even if the animals got only a few laps before it froze again.

Rose had never seen him look like that, so defeated, void of commands and direction. It created a vacuum, a black space. The less he did, the more she sensed she had to do. Her map had changed again, in perhaps the biggest way.

She had, for almost the first time, a notion of herself apart from Sam.

Except for the first weeks of her life, running on a different farm with her mother and siblings, Rose had always been solitary, apart from the other animals, attached only to her one human. And then to Katie, who now was gone.

In the farmhouse, she had her corner in the unused room, where she brought bones, Katie's sneakers, scraps of food, one of Sam's socks, and sometimes she would retreat there. She'd go under the bed with her few things and curl up with them. In her waking dreams she played, ran with other dogs, rolled in the sun.

It was so quiet now she could hear the sound of her own heart beating. She sat by the window and felt the world was too confusing, complex, immovable. Though she didn't have words to frame this fear and sadness, she had instincts piercing enough to make her feel like the tiniest speck about to be devoured by a sea of snow, ice, wind, and cold.

She listened for sounds from the barn, but there were none. All she heard was the wind and the blowing snow.

She glanced at Sam, who was talking in his sleep again.

EVENTUALLY Sam stirred awake, opened his eyes, grimaced in pain, and pulled himself up.

Sam hobbled slowly, painfully, using a broom as a crutch, over to the window to look out with Rose. The candles had burned down, and it was pitch black outside, a darkness highlighted by the dim lights in the farmhouse.

He knew that all of the animals would soon be hopelessly trapped right where they were, if they weren't already. And there was nothing he could do about it. The tractor was useless, it was impossible to move hay, and even if he could it would soon be covered in snow and ice.

His father and grandfather, both of whom had lost friends to farm accidents, had told him at different times that as much as you loved your farm, sometimes you had to love yourself more.

You had to survive. It was you that kept it going.

He knew that lesson well enough; had just learned it once again. There was no glory in dying alone in this awful storm and cold—that would just mean the end of the farm, the end of two hundred years of hard work on the part of his family, whose very blood was ground into the soil.

As the temperature plunged further, he knew that the animals, unable to move, were losing warmth and energy. The cold alone could kill them, especially without fresh feed and water. But he had to stop thinking about it and get himself some help. This was the fate of farm animals; they did not come first, could not. He had to think beyond this awful storm. He had to save himself and Rose.

He remembered telling Katie that he never thought of Rose as "just an animal" anymore. It was something he would never dare say to another farmer.

IN HER LIFETIME, Rose had never experienced such a scene, such a sense of bleakness. She lay down by the back door and closed her eyes briefly.

In her memory, she was playing in the snow with her siblings. Her mother sat on a mound above, looking up at the sheep, down at her pups. For a moment, Rose stopped playing, looked into her mother's eyes, and her head filled with images as she followed her mother's gaze—to that farmhouse, to that farmer, to the sheep, to the cows, and back to her and her siblings. It was the first time Rose had seen those colors, swirls, those rich and sensual smells, each telling her a different story.

Her mother closed her eyes for a moment, as if to take all of it in, and Rose remembered sensing, just for a second, the loneliness in her mother's love for all that she saw in her vigilance, in her responsibility. It was a feeling that was imprinted on her, that never left her mother and, from that moment on, never left Rose.

Now she felt it again, in this storm, on this farm, with this farmer, and these animals, pressing down on her, and it had the effect of washing away all confusion and pain. And fear.

* * *

Sam fell asleep in a chair in the kitchen by the back door, his head slumped onto the table. Rose felt a need to do her work.

She went out through the dog door to check on the wild dog. She was not so baffled by the snow now and maneuvered more confidently, and with more agility, through the drifts. She was adapting. Snow was blowing off the big barn roofs and piling up all around.

She looked around before going into the barn. The dark shapes of the cows and steers were off to her right, standing by their shelter, covered in snow and ice. She looked up the hill to the pole barn. The sheep, still cowed from the coyote attack, were huddled in a corner of the structure.

She entered the barn through the side door. It was dark and bitterly cold and the wind was pouring through the wooden slats. The rooster and chickens were still in the dark and she could hear their soft clucking as they slept.

The wild dog was lying awake, his breathing labored, in pain, weary, hungry. A picture sprung into her mind suddenly—there was a bag of grain, for the cows, in the barn. She had seen Sam tear such bags open with his knife many times, and the grain poured out into buckets for the steers and the sheep.

She saw herself tearing open one of those bags with her teeth. Then a picture of the wild dog, who might not be able to make it now to the farmhouse, to the food bowl, eating the grain.

She trotted over to the wild dog, heard his weakening heart. She headed to the corner of the dark barn, past the chickens sitting up in their roost, past Winston, who was watching her carefully. Rose got to the bag of grain, and tore into it.

She sensed the wild dog's eyes on her as the top of the bag came open, and rich, sweet-smelling pellets poured out onto the ground. She gobbled one mouthful after another until her belly was so swollen it hurt, and then she ran back over to the wild dog, who was struggling to get up, and vomited the grain on the ground in front of him, the pellets intact. The wild dog leaned forward, licked Rose's face clean, and then sat up to meet her eyes. Then he walked over and ate two or three mouthfuls. Satisfied, Rose squeezed back out through the door, widening the snow passage with her claws, and looked around at the awful and gloomy scene. She heard the coyotes, who had been circling all day and the night before, howling up at the top of the hill.

She had been with Sam, shoulder to shoulder through many farm dramas and troubles, and she felt his distress. She had experienced it many times.

It touched something deep and old within her.

In a sense, it was hers now, as well as his.

ONCE THEY HAD CONNECTED, Rose always knew when Katie was addressing her, and she grasped the loving nature of her words and her tone.

They had a routine. When Rose was not working with Sam, she would come looking for Katie, and Katie would turn to the dog, and ask, "You done with your work?" and Rose would wag her tail and wiggle a bit, then go stand by the boots Katie used for walking in the woods.

"I'm done with my chores, too," Katie would say. "Let's us

girls take a break." Anything that was connected to people, and that involved patterns or routines, quickly became cherished work for Rose. A human being's enthusiasm was apparent—something she picked up on instantly.

After just a few walks together, Rose got to know the coat Katie wore for them, the boots, and the other signals that even Katie didn't know she was giving out—how she looked out the window, glanced at the door, reached for a shawl, checked the thermometer, made sure the stove was turned off.

A glance at Katie's feet would tell Rose what was about to happen, as Rose had become a scholar of shoes. She knew the work boots Katie wore for pasture or farm work, and the hiking boots she wore for walks in the woods. The shiny black shoes meant Rose would most likely be left behind, that there was no work for her to do.

The two were connected by an invisible tether on these walks. Katie never brought a leash—Rose had never been on one, not even to go to the vet—and it was unimaginable that Rose would ever take off. Although tempted, she never chased the chipmunks or deer they encountered. Rose always kept an eye on Katie, as she did on Sam when they were out working. How could she do that if she ran away?

On their walks down the path, Rose would rush ahead, circle back, walk alongside, sniffing and listening for the sounds of the woods—the coyotes, wild turkeys, birds building nests, bats squeaking in their sleep, chipmunks and squirrels cracking nuts, deer eating berries and leaves. The various smells and sounds all brought their news to her.

Every now and then Katie would pick up a stick and toss it. Rose would leap up into the air and snatch and run it back to her. Sam never saw this, never even knew about it. Rose did not play with Sam.

They always walked to the same spot: the stump of a giant oak marking the front lawn of a farm abandoned long ago. In nice weather, Katie would sit and take out some home-baked bread. She would eat a piece, and toss another to Rose. The two of them would sit quietly together for a few minutes and soak up the sun.

"This is as still as it gets, isn't it, Rose?" Katie said once. Something about Katie settled Rose, and although she understood none of them, she loved the words that poured out of her. Katie's tone spoke to Rose as distinctly as any words or narratives, and Rose understood her love, her cheerfulness, the peacefulness of their walks. It was satisfying work for her.

In the farmhouse, toward the end of a day, Rose had begun to sit beside Katie up on the couch, and Katie would speak to her as she stroked her back and neck. Rose never permitted anyone else to do this.

Katie often turned to the dog and said, "It's just us girls," and Rose lay by Katie while she worked on her quilts or knitted her scarves. She sat underneath the computer table when Katie worked there, or on the kitchen floor when she cooked. Over time, Rose came to understand the term "girls" as work, but not the kind that her instincts led her to or that she carried images of. It was new to her, and it was good.

"I never thought I'd see it," Sam would murmur softly when he stumbled across the two of them. He loved seeing "his women" together.

One winter day, Rose had been sitting out in the pasture, watching the sheep. There was an ice storm, and soon the dog was covered in ice. It crusted over her eyes, nose, and fur, and Katie called her inside and made her lie down by a warm stove while she gently brushed the ice out of her coat. Rose had rarely—perhaps never—felt so calm and at ease. And she'd never let another human touch her face. Sam, whom she was profoundly attached to, did not connect with her in this way.

Sam told Katie he thought Rose had changed since she had come, and it was a sweet thing to see. "She's too serious," he said. "She's a workaholic." Katie always had the same rejoinder. "Sam, so are you!" And he knew it was so.

Rose thought of Katie often during the day, even when she was working. But there had been one particular day when she was inexplicably drawn to Katie and followed her through the house, even balking at going outside to work. Katie noticed it right away, and so did Sam. Rose had sensed something wrong, something out of place.

She could smell it, almost see it.

Over the next months, Katie became much more still and quiet, the spirit beginning to drain from her. She did not smell or speak or breathe the same way. Rose did not understand right away. Katie was still there, but in a different form.

One day, Katie lay down in the bedroom upstairs where she and Sam slept, and she did not leave the room again. There were no walks in the morning, or in the evening, no time on the couch. Sam didn't call Rose out to work for some days after that, but left her in the room with Katie.

Rose had the feeling she had when she worked, that there was something to do. She jumped up onto the bed and lay still beside Katie, sometimes for hours.

At first Rose was puzzled. She expected Katie to get up. But soon, she adapted to the new routine, and her map changed once again.

When she woke up each morning, the first thing Katie saw was Rose, prompting an increasingly rare smile. Rose usually lay down alongside her on the bed, eyes open, watching her.

Sometimes, if Katie was calm and at ease, Rose would drift off to sleep. But mostly, she simply watched her, listening to the sound of her breathing, the beating of her heart.

The two became inseparable. Sam saw this and encouraged it. He would leave Rose inside and go do the farm chores and tend the crops himself, unless he had to move the sheep or cows.

Rose noticed his approval. Love was a kind of attention that Rose saw clearly, and responded to powerfully.

Before Katie, work had meant one thing to Rose, but now it meant another thing entirely.

Rose felt the power in Katie's looks and words. She was keenly aware of the illness and loved the attention, and soon, she connected the two.

Katie didn't often feel like talking anymore, not even to Sam. It was too hard when everyone wanted her to be happy, to be better, and she felt she was failing them. Rose wanted nothing from her, was content just to listen. So she did. It became her work with Katie, as important as moving the sheep. Rose, the most energetic and restless of creatures, was a surprisingly gifted listener, focused and patient. She never tired of listening to Katie, focused on her with her ingrained intensity, and she felt increasingly protective of her. When anyone other than Sam came into the room, she would growl, raise her hackles, have to be shushed by Katie or Sam, or even led away.

Often she raised her nose to pick up Katie's scent, read her body. The scent had changed, and Rose understood what the smell meant. It pulled her closer to Katie, made her more attentive. Even when she heard the sheep moving outside—she was always listening to them move—she was drawn to stay close. She sensed that her presence was calming, she saw the look on Sam's face when she lay next to Katie, and knew that this was where she needed to be.

Rose was transformed in that room, alert to every sound, no longer just the frenetic working dog she'd been. She connected with the sickness and pain in Katie—and Katie understood that healing her, helping her, soothing her, had become Rose's purpose.

Rose heard her heartbeat flicker, then race, then slow. She caught the smells and heat of the growing thing, and of the medicines, the change in skin color, the fear and restlessness, the smell of the sweat, the overall disturbance in the body. She saw Katie's spirit weaken. She heard the gasps and cries of pain, the changing rhythm of her breathing. She knew everything that was happening inside Katie's body, reacted to it, lying still, moving closer, licking Katie's hand.

She saw other people, other images, from other times, people in beds, in rooms, in fields, turning to her, to others like her, needing attention, needing the feel of her, the focus of her.

"Please stay," she heard Katie ask her one morning.

She understood the command "stay" and sensed the power of the plea behind it.

When Katie took her in her arms one night, she spoke in words that seemed to contain concern for Rose. Rose watched her closely as she spoke, and wondered at the sadness and affection in her voice. She tilted her ears and widened her blue eyes in puzzlement, wondering if this might be a command for some kind of work.

She stayed in the room, leaving only when Sam called her out and tried to make her eat. She rarely did. Once in a while he tried to get her outside, but she rarely went anymore.

One night, Sam locked Rose in the barn with the sheep and told her to go to sleep. Confused, then alarmed, she barked and whined as she heard people, machines, and noises from in and around the farmhouse. In the morning, Sam finally let her out and she raced upstairs into the bedroom.

Katie was gone. Her scent remained, her spirit, her clothes and shoes, but not Katie herself.

Rose began looking for her, racing through the house, unable to fathom where she'd gone.

After all her fruitless searching, Rose slipped back into Katie's bedroom and crawled under her bed and did not move until Sam finally thought to look for her there.

But the sadness didn't go away. A great emptiness settled over her. Every morning, Rose looked for Katie in the house, on the path, in the woods. Every night, she returned to the house and ran to the bedroom upstairs. She did not find Katie, could not pick up a fresh scent.

Rose had lost some of her purpose.

Katie had become a part of her. But she was not on the farm, not in the farmhouse, not in the woods, with Sam. Like so many of the images in Rose's mind, Katie's slowly began to recede, absorbed into her memory, fused with the other images in her consciousness. And she adapted, as she always had. She never left Katie, yet she almost reflexively moved on.

Now Rose went for the same walk almost every morning, and every afternoon, by herself. And each day, she lay down by the stump and waited for Katie to bring her some bread, though she never came.

It didn't matter that she didn't ever find her. Rose would look for her every day for the rest of her life, and perhaps beyond. Sometimes she dreamed of Katie, dreamed of walking in the woods, sitting in the kitchen, lying under the sewing machine.

* * *

SAM HAD KNOWN after the first doctor's visit that Katie would not live long.

At first, he was surprised by Rose's attachment to his dying wife, but when he thought about it, it made sense. One way or another, Rose seemed to know everything, and there was no limit to her faithfulness. He had also witnessed her growing connection to Katie. Of course Rose knew, and of course she would be there.

And so, as often happened, he got out of Rose's way and let her do her work. He had never been good with words or emotions, and although his love for Katie was deep, he almost never knew what to say. Even though he knew better, he couldn't help trying to cheer Katie up, to reassure her. But she was too smart for that, he knew, and there was no good news, would not be any.

So he was increasingly grateful to Rose, whose presence put no pressure on Katie. She gave her nothing but love and relief and companionship as he tended to the farm. As Katie's illness worsened, Rose's grasp of her work with Katie only seemed to grow. By the end it was an astonishing and powerful thing to see.

Katie was worried about Rose, and told Sam so. She took on so much, she said. Would she be broken in spirit? Would she feel as if she had failed? Would she know she had done her best?

Sam tried to reassure her. She's a dog, he said. A wonderful dog, but still a dog. They move on. It's their way.

Later, he regretted locking Rose in the barn when Katie passed away. He had meant to shield her, protect her from seeing her beloved Katie die, to make sure she didn't think she had failed. But it had been a mistake. Sam had always made certain Rose saw all of the comings and goings on the farm.

That was how she kept her map. But now he feared Rose would never stop looking for Katie, would always think she was coming home.

And in this he was correct.

Now Rose kept vigil for Sam on this awful winter night.

She saw his anguish and hurt while he lay on the couch, saw that he was worse, damaged in some way, and in great pain.

But the images that kept recurring to her now were of the lamb being hauled away by the coyotes and the ewe calling to her for help. The danger was outside. And it was getting light again.

Rose heard a bellowing. The cows. She had barely paid attention to them, she had been too distracted by the coyotes and Sam. Rose had seen that animals reacted to cold differently. Sheep, with all of their wool, huddled together for warmth. Cows, with their big exposed sides, had to keep moving to escape the cold. She had seen them during other storms, circling, moving, staying out of the wind.

She went out the back door of the farmhouse, around to the other side of the barn—an easier path, protected from the wind—and squeezed through the gate. Brownie was lowing softly, with three cows standing still next to him, out in the open. Rose saw that the shelter where they usually went in cold weather had collapsed under the weight of the snow.

She started to go get Sam, then stopped, an image of him gasping in pain flashing in her mind. She could sense that several of the cows were barely breathing.

Rose could hear from their hearts that one was dead, frozen to death in place, and the others were weakening.

They had to move.

Though she was exhausted herself, she lunged through the snow and threw herself on one of the cows' haunches, biting. The cow bellowed and spun, and crashed into the other two, startling Brownie and the others, the three of them stampeding in a circle, through the snow, around the wreck of their shelter, overturning a frozen feeder with some hay stuck inside.

She charged again, nipping the smaller cow on the nose, drawing blood. She could hear their hearts racing, feel the blood moving through their bodies. Brownie was the first to see the overturned hay and trot over to it. Rose was too busy watching him to notice the cow behind her lift her heavy front hoof, then swing it rearward, crashing into the side of her head.

TEN

ROSE LAY IN A BLACK FOG, HER HEAD SWIRLING, SPRAWLED ON top of a mound of snow.

She had never been so completely cut off from the sensory tools by which she lived, and soon the pain of breathing heavily became nearly unbearable, her ribs hurt so badly. Her head ached from the blow of the cow's hoof. She began kicking, then barking reflexively, more and more weakly, until she stopped completely.

She closed her eyes, breathed more slowly, and tried to understand what was happening to her. She could not comprehend the sea of black she seemed to be floating in, the blurred images in her head, the sound of her weakening heart, the dark cloud that had enveloped her.

Rose understood time only in terms of dark and light, of eating and the rhythms of the farm animals, of morning birdsong and the hoot of owls and the yipping of coyotes. Now she was totally disoriented, her markers and senses useless. The snow and ice had no smell, and she was much too disoriented to see anything but an inky blackness.

Rose did not panic. Feeling as if she were sinking deeper and deeper into the earth, her resistance turned to resignation.

Death was neither a good nor a bad thing, but a thing all of its own. She sensed death closing in on her, just as she had sensed it enveloping Katie.

She accepted death and dreamed of work, and went into a near trance—a place beyond feeling and fear. Rose did not know how long she lay still, too weak after a time to struggle, unable to move. She was conscious of thirst, of hunger.

She closed her eyes, images moving more slowly now through her mind—her siblings, her mother, the sheep, the farm, Sam. She began to dream. She saw sheep grazing, sheep moving. She smelled animals in the woods, buds on trees and flowers, the smell of lambs. She dreamt of heading off belligerent rams, of walking with the farmer out into the fields, of the sweet feeling of walking the sheep back into the barns and pastures at night, when the sun set, and the farmer closed the gate, and said, "Good job, girl," almost to himself. How warm and good that sounded, and how relieved she felt to have gotten the sheep back safely, to be able to lie in the farmhouse with Sam, to close her eyes, to rest. She heard Sam calling to her, Katie talking to her, saw her own mother licking her fur.

She dreamt of being a pup, of bats squeaking, of bees in the hive, of worms in the ground, and then, a strange dream, a dream of the wild dog, a young dog, moving cows out of a barn, running and nipping and circling. He was a strong dog, confident, with so much energy.

Then she had an image of herself, far away.

The sheep had their heads lowered, settling into the pasture. She looked up, saw the sun beginning to set over the hill. She turned and ran around the flock, in a broad, loping outrun, her tail straight back, her fur blown back in the wind, the sounds and smells of the meadow pouring into her in a stream. Then she turned back toward the sheep. Their heads came up, they turned and began to move back through the pasture, and she was right behind them, driving back and forth—dust, grass, mud in her face, pure joy in every limb and muscle.

After a long run, every last sheep and straggler through the open gate, she would sit down, long tongue hanging. If it was hot and there was a big tub of water, she would climb into it to cool down. She would stay by the gate until Sam came and closed it, which meant she was done. It was as good a feeling as she'd ever felt, and she clung to it now.

She began to feel a release, a letting-go of the pressures of work, of life, of the responsibility, of the worry, and even of the love. She was entering a different place, one with no time, no markings, nothing but rest.

Rose entered a space quieter than she had ever known.

She was on a sandy shore, in the shade of trees. It was cool, at the edge of a vast clear lake whose surface was so smooth she could not see a ripple. It felt like morning, just before the rise of the sun.

Across the lake, there were blue lights as far as she could see, countless lights. She swam across, and it was effortless, as if the water offered no resistance. She almost sailed to the other side, and there the lights enveloped her.

As she drew closer, she saw that the lights were the spirits of dogs. Some were sitting, others waiting, some crossing the water back to the other side. The lights were fluid, porous, dis-embodied, taking the forms of dogs, then lights, then dogs again.

She saw as she swam closer that the other side was filled with woods and meadows, and she heard barking and the songs of birds. Waiting for her on the shore were a female and some puppies, and it wasn't until she glided to the bank that she recognized them.

She saw her brothers and sisters, and with them her mother.

She was a beautiful dog, larger than Rose, with luminous brown eyes, black fur with a white blaze across the forehead, a pure border collie. She was calm, accepting, her tail wagging slightly at the sight of Rose. She was not demonstrative, just calm, loving, welcoming, pleased to see her daughter.

They touched noses, sniffed each other. Rose licked her quickly several times across the side of the nose. Her brothers and sisters were still puppies, and they knew her, and were excited, squirming and squealing and showering her with licks. They were as she had last seen them. And, perhaps, so was she. She didn't know.

Perhaps for the first time in her life, Rose felt a measure of true rest and easiness. She had never imagined anything but work or responsibility, never thought of peace.

Around her, dogs entered the water and swam back and forth across the lake, in animal form on one side, sparkling lights and images on the other. Some were resting, others waiting to cross. They moved back and forth in a timeless pattern. It was almost painfully lovely and hypnotic to Rose. It was richer, more colorful, more nourishing than anything on the farm or in the woods, as much as she loved to run there.

After a few minutes, her mother shooed the puppies away and sat by Rose. The two of them lay down together, and rested quietly. Her mother shared images and feelings and experiences with her.

Rose showed her mother the cruel storm, Sam, Katie, the fear, the coyotes, the death and danger on the farm, in the blizzard, her sense of being overwhelmed and the stirring of choice in her soul. And now, the black and icy fog that suffocated everything—sight, smell, sound, sense.

Rose sensed that her mother shared these images, although she did not offer sympathy or soothing. Rose did not expect it, or even quite grasp the idea. A dog's purpose was to serve, learn, and share, not to comfort or direct. Their spirits were independent of one another, their lives and fates their own.

This was a waiting place, her mother made her understand, where the spirits of dogs came until they were called back. She herself had gone back and forth many times, and so would Rose. They would always meet here, as dogs that were connected to one another did.

It was time for Rose to go back, her mother communicated to her. It was the fate of a working dog—any dog—to be called to serve, and then called again and again. Rest was only temporary. This was a healing place, a place to replenish the spirit and the will, to provide strength and endurance for the harder life on the other side.

A place of reinvention.

Rose felt her mind grow clear, her will and purpose renewed, her instincts sharpened and strengthened.

After some time, her mother got up, touched Rose's nose with her own, and vanished into the sea of blue shimmering, haunting lights that sparkled all around her. The puppies were gone with her.

There was no good-bye.

Rose turned and looked around her, at this beautiful and rich place, filled with smells and lights and sounds and colors— all of her senses engaged, yet peaceful. Then she slipped back into the lake, and glided, rather than swam, back to the other side. Rose sensed, up ahead, the farm and the raging storm waiting for her.

* * *

SHE TRIED to open her eyes, unsure of where she had been, or if she had really gone anywhere. Again she struggled to move, to breathe, but once more gave in to this strange state of resignation, of acceptance. She closed her eyes and all was black again.

Then she stirred.

Suddenly, Rose sensed movement above, felt pressure, heard braying, felt a soft muzzle on her nose. The ground seemed to move as she was pushed roughly to the side.

She was dizzy, confused. Her head was still ringing from the cow's kick. Her ribs ached from landing on the snow, and she was wheezing, wet, every breath a struggle. She shook her head and began what seemed a long climb up and out of a deep hole.

She felt the nuzzle again. She heard a braying. She was being pushed, forced to get up. She opened her eyes and looked into the face of Carol, the donkey.

She and Carol had little to do with each other. Rose did not like donkeys or horses; they were too independent and flighty, and they returned the feeling. Carol had even kicked her once, just like this cow—and tried more times than that.

But now Carol was gentle, encouraging, much as Rose often was with Sam when he fell. The donkey's message was clear. Get up. She had used her warm nose and hooves to move Rose, stir her.

Rose gradually came to her senses, and she slowly got to her feet, looking back toward the cows.

As she returned to full consciousness, she was suddenly back in the storm, on top of the mass of collapsed snow by the barn, trying to get her bearings, trying to grasp where she was, what had happened. But she couldn't, not really. Images streamed through her mind—Sam, the wild dog, the sheep, the storm, the ice, the cows and steers, the goats, Winston.

And then the image of the cows became clear. She turned to see how they were doing, and she heard their hearts beating, saw the steam coming from their noses. They were all right now.

The wild dog came out of the barn and sat behind her. He clambered over the snow, as if to lead her somewhere, and she followed, weakly.

He paused, turned to lick at her bleeding paws, to sniff at her, to push her along gently. She permitted this. He led her to the side of the barn, and through the opening. She followed him in, out of the worst of the wind and snow, and fell asleep on a bale of hay.

Rose did not wonder how Carol had come to walk through the snow and awaken her. Or why. It didn't matter.

WHEN ROSE woke up later she was shaken, drained, startled by what she saw. It was now full daylight, and she was in the big barn. But she had no sense of how long she had been away from the house, in the snow, and then asleep. Every part of her was in pain, especially her sides, which ached with every breath.

It was still snowing, but more lightly now. The wind was quieter. Rose could feel the storm beginning to ebb for the moment, though she knew there was more coming. She could also sense life was still far from normal, for her or the rest of the animals on the farm and in the woods.

Snow had blown in through the sides of the barn. Two or three parts of the roof had collapsed, and debris was scattered across the floor. It was quiet, a dark jumble of machines, feed bags, wet hay, droppings, even rotting eggs. The cold staved off some of the smell and decay. But while the barn was hardly warm, it was still protected from the worst of the wind and snow and ice outside.

It was, for now at least, a refuge for her, a place to regain her energy, prepare for what came next. There was also something close to gratitude, appreciation for the donkey that had somehow awakened her. The blackness had been closing in, and then, just as suddenly, there was light.

Now, she heard a sharp series of cracks from the barn walls—the pipes in the water heating coil system, used to ferry water in the winter, had burst. Just a trickle of water came out, and the animals settled again quickly. Against the cold and wind picking up just outside the barn, the noise seemed minor.

Things in the barn seemed different now. Rose felt the absence of animal movement, shifting, searching for food. It was quiet. Farm animals, especially sheep, were usually wary of Rose, but today there was the absence of fear. The animals—the chickens, the cats, and a cow that had squeezed in through the open door—were all looking at her, which was unusual. Her map seemed to sharpen.

Either she had changed, or all of the animals were reacting to her differently.

Rose had no real relationship with these animals—the cats, chickens, cows. Unlike sheep, they were more independent sorts and rarely needed to be herded or moved. Usually they seemed as confounded by her as she was by them. But here she was in this new reality, inside the barn in the middle of a raging storm with a mix of creatures who almost never would be found together in such close quarters.

It was strange, if not unprecedented, this curious gathering. How odd it would appear to Sam if he could see it. The different species of the farm coexisted, but they were always in their own predictable places, always with their own kind, steered there by some kind of self-awareness that was at the limit of Sam's, and most people's, understanding of animal consciousness.

Sam would have been amazed by a number of curious things. He would have seen Rose and the wild dog lying next to each other, licking each other's wounds, cleaning each other's fur, joined in a bond that only the two of them shared.

In the rear of the barn, Brownie, the steer, had stuck his head in through one of the barn windows, blown open by the wind. He was reaching in to eat from a dwindling bale of hay, the other bales too far from the window for him to reach. Like the sheep, the cows and steers had no food, all of the feeders now shrouded in snow and ice.

Sam would have seen the cat Eve lying near Winston, purring softly as the pompous rooster circled beneath the roosting hens. Inside the barn, the chickens still had some feed, but that was dwindling as well. And the chickens would never venture outside in a storm.

The water buckets were all frozen. Snow blowing in from the windows was spreading across the floor of the big barn, which was dark with the power out, but brightened by the reflected light of the snow.

A few barn swallows had taken refuge in the upper reaches of the barn. Rose looked up now and then as a mouse dared to make a move across a hay bale.

It was the wild dog who seemed to most need her time and attention. Rose sensed he was weakening further. He lowered his head, and, in that dank and cold place, she felt a chill and began to tremble. The moment became theirs, in the way of dogs, in their particular kind of language, beyond the awareness of people. The wind still blowing, they sorted through the smells in the barn, the sounds of mice and rats crawling in the corners.

There was a sadness about the wild dog, a sense of gravity. Even covered in burrs, sores, and wounds, he was a handsome, proud dog, weary of his life alone, without work or purpose.

This farm was the wild dog's now, too. As long as he was able, he was grateful to once again have work. He had an innate respect and affection for this intense little dog. She was dutiful, serious, and smart, as he had once been—as he would be still while he lived.

Rose was not so old, had not been through the same things. But in a way, she and the wild dog were peers now. Out on their own, living off their instincts, without human direction, and so much work still to be done.

ROSE, STILL SHAKEN, made her way through the snow and ice to the farmhouse to check on Sam. She found him still on the sofa, sitting up and cradling his arm. She watched as he took more pills from the bottle near the table, and after that, he nodded off into a fitful sleep again.

When she returned to the barn, she found it quiet, the chickens clucking and sleeping, the big steer munching on hay, the day edging along, even though the difference between day and night had become almost irrelevant in the fury of the blizzard.

Rose could feel that the storm was vast, and not nearly over.

The sheep, calling out from the pole barn, were already

restive, hungry. The ewe was still calling out for her lost baby. The coyotes would surely return, hungrier, better prepared, strong and in greater numbers. The foxes would be hungry as well.

By evening, the animals would be looking in earnest for food and water. There would not be any. The sheep would require her presence, to keep them calm, perhaps to fight off the coyotes. And they would expect her to lead them to food as she did every other day of their lives.

The barn seemed suffused in soft light, a light warmed as if by the blood of the animals themselves. The wood, roof, and pipes in the barn all groaned, creaked, and hissed in a strange symphony, but the animals looked to Rose, sensing she was the leader.

Brownie stopped eating, the goats stopped complaining, the chickens opened their eyes in their roosts and tilted their heads, cocked their eyes at Rose as if awaiting some instruction from her. The wild dog sighed, raised his head. Eve lay down in front of her. The swallows quieted in the rafters, and even the anxious cries and howls of the coyotes up on the hill seemed to grow softer.

Rose was unnerved by the attention and focus. She did not know what was expected of her. The images racing through her mind slowed, changed, calmed. For a moment the storm simply *was,* and it seemed almost beautiful, and timeless.

Rose and the animals sat in this way for a long time.

BUT AS QUICKLY as this quiet had descended, life returned. The mood shifted once again, and this time of communion, of reflection, was over.

Cold, hunger, fear—all began to insinuate their way back

into Rose's consciousness. Rose, like the other animals, was about life. Whatever had just transpired in the barn, all of their instincts were adamant about one thing: survival.

As the morning wore on, the wind shrieked, the snow thickened again, the cold infiltrated through the cracks and crevices of the barn. The mice started skittering around, and the animals returned to their natural manners. Eve vanished into the rafters; Brownie began hungrily seeking hay again; and Winston once more sounded his ear-shattering crowing.

Around midday, Rose heard a pop, then a hiss. She trotted outside and looked up to see a bright-blue ball shoot up from the farmhouse far into the sky. It burned more brightly than any moon or sun or star, and all she could see was that it came from the porch. She could not fathom what it was, but she watched it, transfixed, as it rose higher and higher and burned ever more brightly, even through the clouds and snow.

The sheep began bleating, and she turned away from it, listening as it hissed its way back down to the ground, far out in the woods.

Rose's mind raced, a jumble of confused images, none of which really seemed to fit. There was no pasture, no hay in the feeders, no water in the troughs. No Sam on his machines to move things around.

Rose looked for Sam, where her direction came from, where work began. She lowered her head for the long and tiring climb over the drifts to the farmhouse. Every step was difficult, and her coat was covered in snow, her eyes crusted, her breathing still painful as she worked her way toward the house, the wind blowing straight into her face.

She was well outside the gate when she heard the wild

dog's warning growl from far behind her. She looked up and was surprised to find herself face-to-face with three coyotes, surrounding her in a circle.

The coyote she knew was not among this group, and, looking into their eyes, it was instantly clear to her that they had not come for the sheep or the chickens. They had come for her. They were hungry, determined, deployed in killing mode, and began to howl and bark, signaling to one another that they had found a kill, they had found food and were now calling to the others for help.

Rose did not calculate odds. She could run or fight—but she had never run, not from a sheep, or a ram, or a cow. She would not even have known how to do it. Standing her ground was simply what she did, and she lowered her ears and bared her teeth as one of the coyotes met her eyes in response.

She knew the attack would come from the other two, that his role was merely to keep her focused, toward him. She prepared to fight and was as startled as the coyotes at the loud bang and flash of light that erupted from the farmhouse window. Almost before she could move, the coyotes were in flight, up the hill and into the woods.

Sam shouted something from the window behind her, and she turned to get her bearings. Then she bounded to the back door of the farmhouse, and into the kitchen, where Sam, swathed in slings, limping, his face twisted in pain, was standing with his rifle by the back door.

SAM'S HEART was racing, the adrenaline pumping hard enough that it masked some of the pain in his arm. He'd stepped outside to scan the horizon for the rescue he hoped was coming in the wake of his flare. There, he'd seen Rose face-to-face with three coyotes. Once she was inside, he told her to stay. She lay down and closed her eyes to rest. She was awakened when he got up and stumbled to the back door.

"Rose," he said. "I've got to get out there. I've signaled for help, which means I'll be gone for a few days at least. But I've got to get some more hay to the animals. They'll starve if I don't get some food out to them."

She watched as he threw a parka over his shoulders amidst groans of pain. She followed him to the back door and stood in the doorway.

"Rose, get out of the way," he said. "I have to get out there. I can crawl if I have to—"

Sam had come to see Rose as an extension of himself. He rarely even had to give her a command—she often anticipated him, but when he did, she responded instantly. He loved her for it.

Now, he was shocked by what he saw. Rose was standing, her head low, almost in a working crouch. She was uttering a low growl, her teeth were bared. She was not moving.

At first he thought she must be reacting to something behind him, or something she saw or heard outside. But he looked—no, she was looking right into his eyes. She was growling at him.

He finally managed to sputter, "Rose! What are you doing? Bad girl! Get out of my way. What's wrong with you?"

He yelped in surprise as Rose lunged forward and nipped at his left hand when he tried to reach for the doorknob. He staggered back, and the door fell closed. When he reached out again, Rose went for his hand again. Sam shouted and fell back once more.

"Rose! Let me out. What's wrong with you? Did you get

bit by something rabid?" Each time he opened the door, she lunged at him, growling and snapping.

For a long time the door remained closed, and then he managed to open it a crack.

He gave her a long look. He thought maybe she had gone mad. She met his gaze. The two stared at each other for what seemed a very long time.

Sam looked at this creature, battered, matted, and clearly near exhaustion. She lowered her head but met his gaze. She was not mad. She had been with him every step of the way, through every minute of the storm. She'd rounded up the goats and cows when they had run off, she'd contained the sheep. He was surprised to notice the swelling on the right side of her head, a bump as big as a pear. Something had kicked her or fallen on her.

And she had dug him out of the snow. He would be frozen, dead, in the snow if not for her. He remembered calling out to her, and somehow she had heard him. Now she was telling *him* something. He owed it to her to listen.

Sam remembered her faithful love of Katie when she was sick. Rose was not only an animal he needed to run the farm, she was all he had.

Looking at her eyes, runny from the snow and ice blowing into her face, he knew there was no way she would quit or back down. He couldn't ever strike at her. And he could see that she was clearly taking a real beating working in the storm, something he had been too absorbed in his own troubles to fully notice.

Soon they both would be heading out, away from the farm. He had to accept that. He couldn't leave her in this awful mess.

Rose did not waver. She was silent so long as he was still,

but if he moved forward an inch, the growl rose from her throat. She is not letting me out, he thought. He looked at the blood on his hands, the blood on the sling, felt the awful pain in his arm and leg. He remembered his grandfather: Love the farm, but love yourself, too.

He closed the door and hobbled back into the house, where he lay down on the sofa. "Okay," he muttered. "We'll wait for help."

Rose did not understand what he said, but she recognized the resignation, the submission. She waited until he was settled back on the sofa before returning to the barnyard on her own.

ELEVEN

THERE WAS A BREAK IN THE STORM LATE THAT AFTERNOON, AN interruption in the heavy falling snow—although the killing cold was, if anything, worse.

Rose's ears pricked up at the sound of a powerful, thumping engine. The sound came from above and was still very far away. In her mind she connected it with Sam. She left the barn and began climbing over the drifts, stumbling back toward the farmhouse.

Her paws still hurt. Her head hurt even more. Numerous different images rushed through her mind, conflicting concerns. The cows and steers might still freeze, right where they stood, if they didn't move or eat. The night before they nearly had. This image was shoved aside as the chop-chop sound of a helicopter drew closer, deeper into the valley, through the mist and fog and snow. It was heading straight for the farm, and Rose locked on to it.

* * *

SAM HAD BEEN thinking about the flare ever since he'd shot it off, wondering if it had been seen. By now, Sam guessed that his arm had become infected. He hoped he wouldn't lose it. Shooting pains and fever were spreading through his body. Earlier that day, during a brief break in the storm that had coincided with the agreed-upon time for sending up such signals, he had crawled out into the front yard with his flare gun and launched the little rocket into the sky, trailed by a column of smoke. He knew that other farmers would be looking for the flares, and also that choppers might be circling over the trapped and isolated farms, looking for signals. If it didn't work, he planned to try again in a few hours.

Sam had attempted to pack an overnight bag. He tried to stay awake through the drowsiness and the chills, and kept calling out to Rose to come in. There was no way he was leaving her alone on the farm; she would come with him. But if anything went awry, he wanted to make sure she wasn't without food. So he used his good arm to pull a huge bag of kibble off the shelf and dumped it by the back door, the dog door, so that she would have food if somehow they got separated. The effort cost him, and took him a long time.

But this was just to put his mind at rest. He was determined to get her to leave. She would mind him. She always had. Except for that morning.

WHEN THE HELICOPTER appeared across the valley, the animals heard it long before Sam did. As it got closer, it dropped rocket flares and crackling fireworks to alert Sam to its arrival. The engine noise made the animals anxious, the booms frightened them. Rose herself jumped at the sudden bangs.

She ran to the back door, anxious, unable to sort out this

new happening. She came in under the overhang, pushed open the swivel door, and was startled at the pile of dog food on the floor, and the bowls of water, one of them already covered with a thin sheen of ice. With a low growl, she went looking for Sam, her ruff standing on end.

He was waiting by the front door, holding a bag loosely with his good arm, and Rose took in the heat coming off him, the sweat and confused demeanor. She could spot a sick human or animal instantly. He was disoriented, not himself.

The engine sound drew closer, until it seemed it was hovering right over the house. Rose cowered, barked, and backed up a bit, until Sam called to her, urging her forward.

The huge green chopper looked to Rose like some monstrous and menacing bird. It descended in a roaring whirl, snow blowing everywhere as it approached the front yard, hovering low over the ground.

Sam was standing in the doorway, shielding himself from the rotor blast and blowing snow. Outside in the front yard, a ladder dropped down right out of the sky. The chop-chop sound was almost deafening to Rose. These kinds of sounds unnerved her, but Sam was calling, yelling to her to come. She saw the pale-yellow look of his face, his red-rimmed eyes, the smell of pain and worry on him.

In her seven years of life, Rose had always come when Sam called her. Maybe once or twice she hadn't heard him, when she was in hot pursuit of a ewe or ram—or a tractor on the road—but when she heard, she had always obeyed.

Until now.

SAM LOOKED her right in the eye and said in a loud, clear voice, "Rose, come. Come to me. Right now. I'm hurt. We can't stay here. If I don't get out now, I won't get out. Rose, come. We have to go."

It was at that moment, for the first time, that it occurred to Sam that Rose might not leave the farm.

He knew that she was frightened when she saw a ladder fall and two men in blue clothes, green helmets over their faces, dropping suddenly into the front yard. She growled and barked and whirled, then lunged, probably not recognizing them as people, trying to drive them off. Sam told her to be quiet, get back.

Sam held his good arm out to Rose, pleaded with her, ordered her, turned to the two men and begged for time. He told them he couldn't leave the dog. They looked up at the sky, the swirling, gathering clouds, then shook their heads and moved toward him. Each stood on one side of Sam, one taking his good arm, carefully guiding him, gently but firmly, out onto the porch. He was in so much pain he could not even think of resisting.

He saw the great drifts of snow blowing all over the yard and then turned back to his dog, cowering from the rotor.

"Rose," he said. "Come. Please." There were tears in his eyes, something he'd felt only a handful of times in his life. He thought of Katie. He saw Rose cock her head in puzzlement. She moved a few feet back, edging toward the rear door. He knew then, from the look in her eyes.

"Wait," he yelled to one of the Guardsmen, shouting over the roar, "I forgot my wife's photo. I have to take a picture. Katie. It's right there." He pointed to a photo of Katie on the hallway table. "I've got to take it. I have to have something of hers," he pleaded.

One of the Guardsmen nodded, then ran to get it.

Rose backed away, out of reach, watching as the Guardsman put the photo into a side pocket and jogged back out to Sam. Sam paused again and called to Rose one more time. "Come here, dog, let's get you out of here." But she growled, showed her teeth, then backed into the living room, well out of reach.

Sam looked around, trying to absorb what was happening. Clouds of snow blew around in swirls, the chopper's thunk-a-thunk drowned out almost every other noise, and Sam felt as if he were trapped in a nightmare. He guessed he was.

For Rose, it was all confusing, strange, and frightening.

But Sam saw that something was different.

Rose had heard him call out Katie's name, and she had become calmer, more focused, as if this were a command she understood. As if she suddenly comprehended what was happening, how to work for him.

Rose seemed to make a decision. She turned, backed away, disappeared deep into the house. Sam was surprised. He could only guess that she was getting away from the noise of the helicopter.

He called to her again, and when she returned, he saw that she was holding something. She did not bring it to him. She simply dropped it in the living room, away from the door.

Then Sam realized what it was: one of Katie's sneakers, the kind she always wore on her walks in the woods with Rose. Was it for him?

Sam called to the Guardsmen, but they kept guiding him out onto the porch. Then he shouted, and pointed, and one of them ran into the house and picked up the sneaker.

Rose had stopped growling and trembling now, no longer

cowering or backing up. But she remained out of reach, simply watching Sam.

"Rose," Sam yelled. "Thank you."

He began to plead with her, a tone Rose had never heard before, and she tilted her head to make out the sounds more clearly. "Come. Please. Come with me."

Sam could not command her now, he knew that. He could only ask.

Finally Sam turned to the two men, who were pulling him into a harness, strapping it around his torso, bracing his arm. They had already pumped some morphine into him, and he was beginning to feel it.

"She won't come," he yelled. "She'll never leave the sheep, she'll never leave the farm." But the two men were no longer interested in Rose, and soon he was strapped in. *I am losing everything,* he thought. *I've already lost Katie. And I will never see this dog again.*

He shook his head, tried to collect himself.

"Rose, I'll be back. As soon as I can. I left food." He felt foolish, embarrassed—he knew she couldn't understand, but the words escaped him anyway. He wasn't used to showing so much emotion in front of anybody, let alone two men who were strangers.

He pleaded once more with the men to try to get Rose, but they shook their heads. And he knew they'd never catch her if she didn't want to be caught.

He understood now that she would never get on the helicopter, not alive.

This time her gaze met his, and the two creatures, farmer and working dog, looked into each other's eyes. Neither one had the language, the words.

As he left the ground, tears streamed down his cheeks. He

held up his arm, clutching Katie's sneaker. "Take care of yourself. Take care of things."

And then, simply: "Rose."

THE LAST of Sam that Rose heard was his weakening calls of her name as he vanished up into the sky, something beyond her comprehension.

If he had not imagined her refusing to come along, she had never imagined his leaving this way.

Rose had seen tears in his eyes, and she had cocked her head again in puzzlement. She could smell his sadness through the snow and wind.

Rose was usually sure of her world, but some things happened that she could not begin to grasp.

As the helicopter pulled away, the snow settled, and the roar became fainter, she ventured up to the front window to look in wonder. The sound of the machine changed as it began to move away from the farmhouse, taking the biggest piece of Rose's world with it.

She looked around her. As the helicopter receded into the distance, the place became still again. Sometimes, when Sam left in his truck, the farm settled like this, as if part of its soul had fled. But this stillness did not seem familiar or routine. Sam had vanished, eaten up by the sky and the storm.

Now, there was only the sound of the wind, the snow falling on creaky roofs; now she knew an emptiness, a stillness that she had never experienced before. Overwhelmed, she lay down, as if struck by the sudden sensation of being alone. She was still, her eyes half closed, her nose down, trying to get her bearings.

She thought briefly that Katie might be upstairs, but she heard and smelled nothing.

Her head came up. The pull of work stirred her.

There was a lot to do.

Rose went back into the kitchen, wolfed down some food, gulped some water, and sat again, listening. All she heard was silence. The forest and woods were still, and even inside the house she felt the cold as the wind began to howl again and the snow began to fall more heavily.

Sam was gone. He was not there for her to worry about, follow, keep track of. He was not there to support, direct, command. Rose did not know loneliness, but she felt alone in a different way than she had ever experienced.

Defying Sam had been new and strange to her, and somehow frightening. She had never done it before; it went against her nature, her instincts, everything she had known and learned. It had torn her in half. She was as surprised by it as Sam had been. It changed things. Yet it was clear, simple in its own way.

She could not leave the farm. She could not go with those people, not leave the sheep and the cows. And Katie.

Her map, her senses, her mind, all of it was a jumble. The stories in her head were not of being alone. They were not of the incoherent experience of having no direction, no context, no others. She had no images for this.

She stopped, looked to the front door, and then climbed up the stairs and into the bedroom where Katie and Sam had slept. She went to the other sneaker, under the bed, where it always was. She picked it up and brought it downstairs. She wandered with it a moment, then dropped it on the kitchen floor and sniffed at it.

Carefully, deliberately, she licked the front edge of it, working her way around the side, taking in the rich smells the moisture revived in it. When she got around to the laces, she chewed through two or three strands, and then pulled one out.

The house was quiet, except for the sounds of snow buffeting the windows, sliding off the roof, the old beams creaking and stirring under the stress of the snow and the wind. Rose chewed slowly and deliberately.

When she was finished, she picked up the shoe and brought it into the living room, where she hid it under the footstool by the old black sofa.

THE SKIES DARKENED and the snow thickened as Rose made her way back to the barn. She turned to look up at the sky, hoping for a glimpse of Sam, some sense of where he had gone, whether he might be coming back down again, but there was none.

Inside the barn the wild dog came up, still limping, to greet her. The once-more insolent cats were slinking around, the goats were calling out to her, the chickens were pecking for fleas and crumbs and bits of hay and grain.

She plowed through the snow in the opening of the side barn door, burrowed and dove her way up the hill again to the pole barn. Two or three times she was almost halted by the wind and snow, blowing with renewed fury into her face.

The sheep were anxious, up and moving about, hungry, edgy, close to panic. They were so frightened that few of them even seemed to notice Rose, or lift their heads, or back up as they always did when her eyes met theirs.

Rose knew the consequences if she did not keep the sheep calm. One or two, then others, would panic, scatter, run off into the cold to die and freeze, or into the waiting jaws of the coyotes. Their only safety, their only warmth, was to stay together where they were.

Now inside the relative shelter of the pole barn, she lay down.

Here, more than ever, she needed to focus, to collect herself, but the images in her head came and went too quickly. It was a baffling time. So much to do. So little she *could* do.

SHE HEARD THE wild dog barking urgently from the barn, heard a frantic braying. She looked down toward the barn and saw the wild dog barking, and Carol, who was lying on her side, crying out in panic, struggling to get up, unable to stand in the snow and ice.

Rose rushed down the hill.

Carol was now lying still, disoriented. Rose moved closer and listened to her heart.

It was clear that Carol was beginning to go into shock, something Rose had seen the sheep and cows do when they were terrified or trapped, slipping into a kind of paralyzed, semiconscious state. Usually, death followed quickly, and Rose could see, even from a few feet away, that Carol was shutting down.

She saw from the tracks that Carol had come up the hill from the barn and then slid back down, getting herself wedged between a mound of snow and the outside wall of the barn. She was almost upside down, a terrifying and helpless position for any animal, and Rose could see her fear and confusion.

The wild dog was standing above her. This was not, Rose could see, in his experience. Nor was it in hers. But he had called to her, had brought her running.

Rose looked to the wild dog. She looked at the barn. She

looked back to the house. She called upon her memory. But she had no notion, really, of what to do, no training to fall back on. She hesitated, listening to Carol's frantic braying, her hooves thumping against the barn, bloodying her ankles and legs. Rose had to settle her down.

Rose crawled and slid down the embankment, trotting around to Carol's head. The donkey was alternately quiet, then flailing, frantically trying to find purchase so as to right herself. Thick clumps of snow were falling on her from the roof, sliding down the hill on top of her.

Rose barked once, to get her attention.

Carol was startled, but she turned her head to look into Rose's eyes. Rose saw things in Carol's eyes she had never seen before—her dreams, her memory, her weariness, the pain in her old legs. She saw things that only animals see in one another. They were different, these two, yet there were things that connected them, and some connection was being forged now as each met the other's gaze.

Carol was an old girl, she had suffered much, seen a lot, and, looking into her eyes, Rose saw some of Carol's life rushing between the two of them. She saw sadness, but she also saw acceptance.

Rose moved closer. She was trying to calm Carol with her look, and within a minute or so Carol stopped flailing. She continued watching Rose intensely, as if her very life depended on it, as if this were the comfort she needed to steady herself and go where she was to go. Rose still had no notion of how to help Carol get up, sandwiched as she was between the tightly packed snow and the smooth wall of the barn. She could not help as the donkey had helped her. Carol seemed to know it, too.

Until now, they had always been viscerally wary of each

other, two very different creatures, even though there was a sense of being in the family of the farm, in Sam's care. But just hours before, they had crossed a line together, and Carol knew her life was now in Rose's care.

Among Rose's keenest instincts was a deep understanding of what she could and could not do, but there was no experience for her to draw on now, no skill to use, no battle to fight.

Rose lowered her head, listening. She could hear that Carol's heart was beating slowly and would soon stop. Rose knew this thumping sound well. She knew when a sheep was close to death, usually well before the sheep even sensed it.

Carol's heart was very faint, hard even for Rose to hear above the wind.

The cold had weakened her. The storm was wearing down her tired old body. Rose saw it for what it was: simply the way of things. Rose had no strategy for fighting that.

Meeting Carol's gaze, Rose saw the spirit draining out of her, drifting up into the snowy sky—a blue streak, a vapor, an impulsion of light and energy.

Carol snorted, brayed softly. Rose, squinting against the snow and the wind, leaned forward to sniff Carol's forehead, gently. Carol leaned her head to the side, one eye covered by snow, only one free, to look at Rose, meet her eyes.

Rose had her own animal notion of separation, of good-bye. She had only a sense of what it meant. Carol had always given off a feel of aloneness, and Rose could smell much pain in her.

It was clear to Rose that Carol was saying good-bye to her, the only creature on the farm she had chosen to communicate with. Rose saw, in the colors and reflections of Carol's eyes, where images were stored and passed on, images from the old donkey's life. She saw the early images of Carol's life, much as she recalled her own—the donkey's mother, her brothers and sisters, playing in a pasture, grazing in a field. She saw Carol and two of her sisters running through an open field as fast as they could go, kicking up their hind legs, braying with joy.

She saw the suffering that came later—the loss of work, the loneliness, the hunger and neglect, eating the bark of trees and weeds, drinking from rancid rainwater, from the dew on grass, standing out in the open in rain, storms, cold, and heat.

She saw the beatings, the hunger, attacks by dogs, and she smelled and sensed the pain, the ticks and flies and sores and the aching hooves and joints, and then, the change: the safety of Sam's farm, hay and shelter and grain, peace and quiet.

She saw Carol's disinterest in the cows, her love of the sheep, her fear of Rose herself, who was, to her, just a different kind of coyote, a predator in her own right, one more carnivore to be wary of.

Rose had seen that Carol was mostly left alone, and given no work, and in that time she found her easiest and most peaceful days. All this flashed in the light of Carol's eyes, and Rose could see it clearly, and understand it well.

Those reflections were Carol's farewell, her own kind of good-bye.

And then, as Rose knew it would, Carol's body grew lifeless, her eyes vacant, her spirit now gone. What was left was smell and flesh, none of which held any meaning for Rose.

The wild dog watched, quiet.

Rose looked over at him, then she sniffed Carol's body one last time. So did he. The snow was already forming on Carol's head, and across her body, which had stopped heaving.

Rose's map had changed once more.

Something inside of her stirred, moved her forward. If she was accepting, even passive, about a natural death, she felt quite differently about life, which was calling to her from everywhere around her to do her work.

ROSE TURNED and looked up toward the sheep, then climbed wearily back up into the pole barn. She was tired, but a part of her also felt new. She was moving from thing to thing, gaining certainty.

The sheep were still clustered by the rear of the barn, protected from the wind and heavy snow by the three-sided barn and its overhang. The coyotes, she sensed, were up at the top of the hill, waiting. She did not know where the foxes were. She heard nothing from the forest or the woods. The water troughs in the barn were frozen.

Rose realized, very suddenly, that her map had not included most of the cows or the steers. Her instincts drew her out of the pole barn and to the rear pasture, which she could reach only by going through the big barn and back out the side door.

She paused there. She could see that some of the cows were again struggling, almost frozen in place. The high drifts and ice had trapped them, the lack of food had weakened them, and the brutal cold and fierce winds had pulled the heat out of them.

Only Brownie and a handful of cows, huddled by the rear door, were still moving, their breath steaming out of their noses. Brownie was shifting back and forth, his huge body a windblock for the cows, who were leaning into one another, waiting patiently for the hay that came from the barn doors.

The steers and cows were never allowed into the barn—it wasn't big enough for them—and so Sam had built a sun-and-rain shelter for them away from the barn, enough protection against anything but a storm like this. The shelter roof had collapsed under the weight of the snow, and the drifts had piled up so high around it that the cows and steers couldn't even use its remaining walls as protection against the wind.

When Brownie looked at Rose and bellowed, it seemed like a distinct call for help. Rose looked him in the eyes. She felt as desolate as the farm looked.

Rose passed the pump and spigot that Sam turned on twice a day to bring water to the barn. She studied it for a few seconds. Often, she had been distracted by the sound of an engine kicking on in the barn. Sam called it a generator, and it was kept for emergencies, a small, propane-driven machine that provided heat and light to the tool room in the corner of the barn, and to one of the deicers that was now trapped in a frozen water trough. Sometimes, when there were storms, and the house went dark, it came on and water emerged from the pump. In her mind, Rose made a connection between the machine and the water, but could not go further.

She simply didn't understand, didn't know how to make the water come. There were no images in her head, nothing in her experience or memory to draw from. For the first time, she felt something close to frustration. She understood there was water in there somewhere, but she had no way of manipulating the machine, getting it to do what she wanted. She stopped, stared at the generator again, then at the pump.

She watched it a bit, then sniffed it, smelled nothing useful. She touched it with her nose, but recoiled from the cold metal. No images came to her.

She had reached a limit, a place beyond her experience. She did not know what to do, so she left the pump behind. She knew the animals were thirsty, but they could go a while without water. They could eat snow, but it drained precious body heat. It was the cold and hunger she feared the most.

She ran back around the rear of the barn and inside. Rose was focused now on the cows—her mind off Sam, no longer puzzling about where he had gone.

She came quickly into the barn and hopped up toward the rear of the old building. There were several mounds of hay piled up on the second floor and gaping holes in the back wall from the wind and the storm.

Remembering how the barn cats moved, she hopped onto one bale, then another, before leaping up onto the hay-storage platform on the upper floor of the barn. It was not a big jump for her.

She grabbed a mouthful of hay and pulled it from a bale, then ran to one of the breaches in the wall and dropped it there on the wooden floor. Then she pushed it through the hole with her nose. It was only a small clump, but she heard the cows outside begin to low and stir, heard them all move toward the hay drifting to the ground. She ran back for another mouthful, pulled it out of the bale, dragged it to the opening, and pushed it out. She did this again and again. She had no sense of how many times she ran back and forth, but it was until there was almost no hay left on the platform, and she looked out and saw all of the cows milling and bumping into one another, quietly eating the hay. There was a considerable amount now, covering a wide swath of snow. In moving and eating, the cows seemed to have revived, gained strength, bought time.

In her mind, images kept recurring.

She had to get the cows and the hay together. And she had to get the sheep to the barn as well.

Rose jumped down off the platform, landing with a thud

right in the middle of the dark space at the center of the barn, causing the quiet space to erupt. Chickens squawked, Winston puffed himself up and began crowing, and the barn cats melted into the upper floor, where dark-green bales of hay were stacked.

Rose nosed the wild dog to call him to work. He could see right away that something was different about her, and he struggled to his feet. The two went to the rear of the barn, to the ancient sliding door that was hanging fitfully off its hinges, leaving a small opening in the doorframe.

The door was more than a hundred years old, and, like most farmers, Sam didn't fix things he didn't absolutely have to fix. The door was never really used, so it didn't matter how loosely it hung. Sam joked that a good wind would turn the door into a sail, and maybe the whole barn would take off across the road, it was so old and rickety.

Because it was on the westward side of the barn, a little less snow had gathered behind it, but there was still too much for a sheep to wade through. The wind was furious in the back, and so was the ice, some of it crusted where the pipes had burst and shot water out the rear of the building.

Rose began chewing at the outermost plank, which was rotten and soft. A large chunk of the wood came off in her mouth. She stuck her head through the hole. Brownie was on the other side.

A bale of hay was behind her. She wanted Brownie to smell it. She and the wild dog chewed off another section of plank and after a few minutes, there was a two-foot hole in the side of the sliding door. It was still far too small to fit a cow, but Rose barked and Brownie's nose came through, as she expected it would.

Rose had seen cows slide barn doors open when they were

hungry and they knew there was hay inside. They were curious creatures, and when it came to food they could be savvy
and quick.

But even Rose did not anticipate the crack and crash when
Brownie's great head came exploding through the hole, taking
four or five planks of wood with it. He only had a few feet to
back up, but it was enough. When Brownie charged the barn
door—drawn by the smell of the hay on the other side—his
2,500-pound frame burst right through it. The door split, and
half of it fell backward into the barn, sending Winston and the
chickens running. Brownie squeezed himself through, and
the four surviving cows ambled in behind him, each hungrily
ripping at the three bales of hay.

Now Rose's mind turned to the sheep. She had to bring
them to the hay, too. A number of them were pregnant, and
she knew they wouldn't survive without food.

Rose led the wild dog on the long hard trek up to the pole
barn, and, once inside, they trotted up behind the sheep. She
examined their weakening stances and confused and hungry
eyes. They had to get down the hill. The sheep and the hay had
to be together.

Rose dove into the back of the pole barn, behind the sheep,
who then moved forward, startled. She lunged at the ewe in
front of her, nipping at her buttocks, her hind leg, her tail,
grabbing the wool from her legs in her teeth.

The sheep had nowhere to go. They were engulfed,
trapped by mounds of snow, and two dogs crowding them
from the rear. They panicked. They raced back and forth trying to get away from the crazy dogs, and then finally fled the
only way they could—straight into the wall of snow that had
piled up in front of the barn.

The two farm dogs, without overt signals or communication, went to work. The sheep were moving downhill, the weight of their own bodies propelling them through the mounds of snow. Rose circled and, where necessary, charged and nipped, bit and pushed. The two dogs put intense pressure on the flock, and they lunged through the drifts toward the back of the big barn.

One ewe, about to go into labor, and too weak from the cold and hunger, would not move. Rose chose to leave her behind. Another jumped into the drift and twisted her leg; Rose heard it snap and break. The sheep fell back and to the ground, struggling to get up, then collapsed on her side in shock. Had Sam been there he would have gotten his rifle and killed her to ease her pain. But in this cold and wind, she would not suffer long.

Rose looked back once at the old ewe, and at the injured one, and then plowed into the snow after the rest of the flock.

The sheep formed a natural wedge, their weight and momentum forming a living plow, creating a furrow through the drifts. Snow flying, they pushed down the hill. Rose had brought the flock down in bad weather many times before, but never through snow this high, wind this strong, or temperatures so low.

The two dogs worked relentlessly. It took nearly an hour for the flock to move those few hundred feet. At some point, the sheep finally smelled the hay and moved on their own, without encouragement.

Eventually, dogs and sheep, almost equally exhausted, broke through.

But here Rose had made a mistake, one of her few. Brownie and the cows were already inside devouring the hay. When the flock of sheep charged through the shattered barn door and rushed toward the food, the cattle spooked.

It was a small area, and when Brownie moved to protect his cows, lunging and kicking at two of the ewes, they were slammed into the side of the barn.

The sheep, in a frenzy, rushed ahead anyway, cracking open several of the stalls, and damaging the shelves inside the barn. It was too much for the cows, and they backed out as the sheep began tearing at the few bales of hay still lying on the floor.

Rose, uncomfortable with any kind of mayhem or disturbance, stepped into the barn, but the hungry sheep and starving mothers were beyond control. She and the wild dog backed off. One ewe began circling, about to go into labor on the floor of the barn, pacing restlessly as the others ate.

In a few minutes, the hay was gone. Brownie and the cows had consumed two bales by themselves, and were now out in the back, already dusted with snow again. Half the sheep were inside the barn, half out.

There was no more hay, except in the upper reaches of the loft, and no way to get to it.

Rose's map was in shambles.

Some of the sheep, exhausted, were lying down. Some milled outside in the snow, still protected by their thick coats. One had died, crushed by the cows. A second ewe had gone into labor, straining. Rose could hear her heartbeat, and the lamb's. She added the baby to her map, removed the sheep killed by the cow.

The cows stood by the rear of the barn with Brownie.

Rose glanced now at the wild dog—he had staggered over to a pile of straw, collapsed, and fallen asleep in a corner of the barn—and tried to get her bearings.

Sam was on her mind. But her sense of Sam and his role in her life seemed muddled. He had left, yet there was still so much work to do.

* * *

Down from the hill, by way of her exquisite sense of smell, came fresh news—coyotes. They were nearby, and they were hungry. Tonight, they would come for the sheep, for the lambs. They would come for her.

Rose looked back up at the hill, for the ewe in labor that had remained behind. She hadn't forgotten, and she turned to begin the trek back up, leaving the wild dog in the barn.

The ewe was still struggling to give birth, circling in the wind and snow, then lying down in a near collapse, drained from cold and hunger. Rose smelled her fear and heard the struggle in her belly.

The ewe's turning had gouged a hole in the snow.

Rose could not hear the heartbeat of a lamb inside of her, though she did hear the ewe's own weakening heart. She listened to her cries, a sound she had heard a few nights before when she had awakened Sam.

Rose circled the sheep, giving her eye, trying instinctively to get her up. This was what Sam always asked her to do during births. Get up, get up.

She thought of Sam, and of his bag, and of the way he reached inside the ewes and pulled out lambs.

The ewe would not get up.

Rose slowed. Circling the ewe was useless.

So was barking or nipping. Her instincts suggested nothing that she might do; neither did her memory. The inside of the ewe, the process of lambing, this was beyond her.

Rose turned to the farmhouse to listen for Sam. He was not there. He was not in the barn. Or in any of the pastures. He was not inside his truck. Rose felt responsible for Sam—more so than she did for the sheep. She could not fathom where he had gone, nor could she stop looking for him.

The ewe, in pain and great weariness, struggled in the snow and wind, fighting with all her energy to get her baby out, calling out to the other ewes for comfort. She looked at Rose and groaned, her cries weakening.

Rose whined softly again and again. Then she quieted. It seemed as if Rose and this mother were alone in a sea of shifting white and cold.

There was nothing else but them.

And the storm.

After some time, with the life seemingly draining from her, the ewe sighed. She was on her side, her eyes open wide.

Rose listened, tilting her ears. She was startled.

She heard the ewe's heart grow stronger, beat more rapidly. Rose lowered her head, now hearing the heart of the lamb as well, beating softly but steadily. All around her, there was the fearful sound of the wind, and the heavy snow hissed as it hit the ground. These sounds unnerved her as the beating hearts transfixed her. In her mind were the powerfully conflicting images of emptiness and life.

Rose barked, then nipped at the ewe's legs, watching as she rose gamely to her feet, slowly and deliberately, groaning and straining—and a moment later a glistening, wet, newborn lamb slid out of her backside and onto the snow, trailing afterbirth in a red, liquid stream.

The ewe, snow swirling all around her, turned to nuzzle the baby, who struggled to her feet and began bleating, already looking for her mother's nipples underneath her ice-encrusted coat of wool. Rose knew she had to get them quickly to shelter, or else they would freeze in the cold and snow. This was work she knew well.

Exhausted and nearly frozen, Rose began to bark, backing up and putting herself between the pole barn and the ewe. The mother, bewildered by the dog's sudden change in demeanor, frantically began nuzzling the lamb down the hill toward the big barn, moving the newborn through the freshly plowed trail the rest of the sheep had made a few minutes earlier. Together, they vanished into the snow and wind.

It was a long trek down in the brutal cold, and Rose could not help them. Lambs would not be herded, and if she came near, both might panic, separate, and disappear into the snow. Rose had no sense of whether the two would make it.

All she could do was stay behind the mother, keep pressure on her to move, and the lamb would follow. But they refused to move in a straight line, were startled by the wind, confused by drifts. Rose had to move on.

She walked down the hill by herself and into the barn. She shook herself off, looked at the chickens clucking softly in their roosts, lay down next to the wild dog, and closed her eyes. The lives of sheep were never predictable, not even to a herding dog. She was tired, more drained than she had ever been.

She heard the wild dog's uneasy breathing, the barn cats moving high up in the rafters, the cows bellowing softly out in the rear pasture. She entered a dreamy state, somewhere between sleeping and wakefulness.

After some time, a sound roused her. It was outside the barn, the opening of the gate. She sat up and growled. The wild dog lifted his great head and bared his teeth as well.

Then she heard a voice calling out to her, faint at first but then clearer, and familiar, but muted by the wind. "Rose, Rose, where are you, girl?"

It was Sam. He had returned.

Rose was beside herself with excitement.

She leaped up, tail wagging, and rushed to the barn door, where she almost ran into Sam, his arm still wrapped up, holding a brown bag in his good arm.

He was on his way to the barn, out of the snow and the mist. She touched his knee with her nose, and then barked furiously, rushing up beside the barn and toward the pole barn to where the stricken ewe had gotten up and given birth, calling Sam's attention to it.

She watched as Sam opened the gate and clambered up the hill, setting down his bag and reaching into the ewe to pull out the last of her afterbirth before leaning over the glistening lamb and wiping her off with his cloth. Sam picked up the lamb in a sling and with Rose pressuring the ewe from the rear, the mother and baby made it into the shelter of the big barn.

Suddenly, she heard Winston crowing, snow falling from a roof and blowing in icy bursts through the barn walls.

Rose opened her eyes.

She was in the barn, disoriented. She shook the fuzziness from her head, then walked to the door, looked out into the storm.

Sam was not there. He was not by the barn, or up the hill. She looked, sniffed, and listened for him.

Then she turned and made her way through the snow and back up the hill toward the pole barn. She could not see the ewe or her newborn lamb.

TWELVE

For the first time in days Rose did not have work to do. Or, rather, she had exhausted the things she could do. She couldn't open doors, turn on faucets, haul hay bales, beat back the storm. She understood this was temporary, a respite.

Out of habit, she looked and listened for Sam, sometimes almost in disbelief at the idea that he was not there, had not returned, that he had inexplicably gone up into the sky and vanished. Sometimes, an image occurred to her of trying to stop the big green bird, but Sam had not seemed afraid, nor had he asked her to help.

Now that Brownie and the remaining cows had gotten some food, they were still cold and weakening, but alive. Several of the ewes were exhausted, but they, too, had eaten a little, and the remaining flock was making its way back up to the familiarity of the pole barn. It would leave them more exposed, at least to the predators gathering at the top of the hill, but it was home for them. They had never lived in the big barn, and they had their own corners, patterns, and smells. In the pole barn they also had space.

Like most animals, sheep did what was familiar. Neither Rose nor the wild dog had the energy to try to keep them all down in the barn, which was a dark, cold mess of snow, ice, wet hay, and broken beams and pipes.

The wild dog, growing ever weaker from the cold and lack of food, was still lying down in a corner. Rose thought about leading him to the farmhouse to eat, but she wasn't sure he had the strength for the journey.

She walked over and saw how thin he was, how shallow his breathing, and she made a decision. She knew that he had to get to the farmhouse or he would die right where he lay. She could see a picture of it in her head, feel the warmth draining from his body, hear his breathing slow, his lungs filling with fluid.

Better to die on the move than curled up in a corner of the barn.

She leaned over, touched his nose, and he opened his eyes, looked into hers; then he struggled, slowly and painfully, to his feet.

He did not know where they were going, but she was his farmer now, his reason, his leader. She was the only thing left that made sense or offered promise to him. She led him to the opening in the door and began the push through the drifts. For him, it would be a nearly unbearable walk, testing his painful limbs and joints, his waning energy and strength.

Rose had forged something of a path on her earlier trips to the farmhouse, but it was a difficult and arduous one for the old dog, already exhausted from his work with the cows and in the barn. His ribs were sticking out, and his gums were a pale yellow. He gave off a scent of sickness.

Rose slowed her pace. One step at a time, then another, then pause, look back, then another step, pause. The first drift was the highest and the hardest, and the rest of the way, she lowered her head and pushed a path through the snow with her chest and shoulders. She saw that he was moving on will alone.

It took a long, cold time, but the two of them finally made it, panting, to the back door. Rose nosed it open and led her companion through.

He stopped and looked at the huge pile of kibble Sam had left and then at her, and when she did not challenge him, he limped over and began to eat the dog food. He took four or five mouthfuls, and it was almost too much for his stomach. He walked over to the bowl of water and drank greedily, and then Rose led him into the living room, where he made his way gingerly over to the dog bed on the floor, nearly collapsing onto it.

Rose followed and sniffed him—heartbeat already stronger. Here, she decided, is where he needed to stay. She did not know if he could or would survive inside, but she did know he didn't stand a chance out in the cold and the storm. She listened to his heart, watched his stomach rise and fall. She said good-bye to him, in case she did not see him alive again.

Rose's understanding of death had been simple for most of her life. Animals died all the time, in the woods or on the farm. She simply removed them from her map. When Katie became ill, Rose could smell the sickness in her—in her sweat, on her skin. She saw that Katie's body was dying; she had seen that before. It was her sudden absence that bewildered her, the loss of her physical presence.

She had never seen Katie leave, and that was why Rose looked for her so relentlessly. She did not want that to happen to the wild dog.

She and the wild dog had connected, almost viscerally, and she knew now what it was to miss someone or some thing she was connected to. Still, separation and death were givens in her world. She did not fear death herself, or even imagine she would die. She imagined now that she would go to the place of blue lights and see her mother again. Perhaps even see the wild dog.

If it was the wild dog's time, it was not her work to fight it or lament it. So she was preparing herself, in her own way, drinking in the smells and memories of what was familiar. She had never heard the farmhouse so still, seen it so dark or felt it so cold.

So lonely.

She walked to the edge of the living room, looked for Sam on the porch, where she had last seen him before he was lifted into the sky, and then looked for Katie in the sewing room. She remembered her life in the house. She remembered the box in the kitchen she slept in as a puppy. She remembered the sofa she lay on while Katie and Sam watched TV. She remembered the bones that they had brought her, the dog bed, Katie and Sam drifting through the rooms like ghosts.

She remembered every sound she had heard in the house—TV, radio. talk shows, conversations, food cooking, teapot whistling, mail coming through the slot, the hissing of radiators, the rumblings from the boilers in the basement, the sound of lights being switched on and off, the water rushing through the pipes, the flies laying eggs on the windowpanes, the settling and creaking of wood, the groaning of the roof in the snow, the damp, the ladybugs, wasps, and bees that built hives and nests, the ants, termites, and beetles that lived in the walls and ceilings, the moths fluttering throughout the house.

To her, the farmhouse was a hive of noise and emotion, people and sounds, sometimes deafening to her, always fascinating. She could lie on the porch for hours, or on the hearth in front of the woodstove, at Sam or Katie's feet, half dozing, listening to the cacophony all around her.

She had always moved about the house at night, run in and out during the day. Sometimes she slept at the foot of Sam's bed, sometimes under the bed, sometimes in Katie's sewing room. Sometimes she snuck out quietly in the middle of the night and went out to the barn to watch over things.

Peaceful memories—soothing. She padded to the front door, lay down, looking once more for Sam, waiting for him to come down from the sky, to tell her what to do, to go out into the barn and bring down hay and turn on the water and save the flock.

She sensed the coyotes gathering on the hill, hungry, even desperate, watching, observing the death and confusion down below. Frightened ewes, weakening cows, a tired old dog, the absence of people, Rose.

She saw the farm as the coyote would have seen it. Prey everywhere, sustenance. The survival of his pack all gathered in one place, and nothing powerful enough to stop him.

They would make a plan; they always did. Unlike Rose, they were many strong, working in concert. They didn't cajole by nipping. They waited until their prey was vulnerable, defenseless, and they overwhelmed with numbers, speed, and fear, killing quickly and savagely.

The coyote had to succeed or his den would face death— which he could not permit any more than Rose could permit the extinction of the farm animals.

They were on the move, she could feel them. In her mind, she could see them, circling, hiding, watching, waiting. The coyote would have gathered his den by now, and they would have spread out all over the hilltop, behind the drifts, in the clump of trees, behind the fence and the big trees.

* * *

ROSE SLID OUTSIDE through the door. She had not adapted to the reality of the storm. Each time she returned to it she was startled by the bleak and frigid landscape. Every time she returned to it, it was different, and she had to reorient herself.

She turned and went back inside, where she found the wild dog lying where she had left him. She lay beside the spent dog, who was breathing slowly, but who lifted his head and turned his eyes to hers. He was giving her permission to go, as they both knew she had to.

He was nearly done.

Rose stayed with him for a few more minutes, both of them listening to the howl of the wind, the snow thumping off the roof, the distant bleating of the sheep.

There was nothing to do now. The two dogs waited together. They both slept, briefly. They each had simple dreams—moving sheep, cows, running through the woods. These dreams were nourishing, reassuring. They called up the history of dogs, of work completed, of successes.

It was night now. The snow was still falling, the wind a little quieter. The farm was buried, impassable.

The wild dog was lying on his side, whining a bit in his dreams, his stomach heaving slowly. Rose looked at him one more time.

Again she touched his nose. At first, this dog was just another creature running in the woods, another danger to the farm, something to be monitored, barked at, kept in check. One afternoon, Rose had looked down from the pasture and seen this old dog looking up at her. Something stirred inside of her—as it used to when she was a puppy with her mother.

He wasn't, then, trying to come into the farm, wasn't aggressive or challenging. He simply stared at her, and perhaps it was then that she knew. Or perhaps it was when she first led him into the barn. Or when he tried to stand by her when she faced the coyotes, and she protected him.

Or only right now, as he lay so peacefully and so accepting, near the end of his life. It was a series of moments rather than one.

She did not know if he recognized her as his daughter, but she had known, on some level, from the first, that he was her father.

THIRTEEN

ROSE LEFT THE WILD DOG ASLEEP IN THE KITCHEN AND MOVED slowly back toward the door, toward the storm. She closed her eyes, put her head down, and plunged back out, moving slowly and deliberately in the direction of the barn.

She heard the goats calling out in complaint from inside their shed. There was nothing she could do for them. They would be eating down the hay Sam had stuffed into their sheds before he'd gotten hurt. She saw Brownie through the mist and snow, breath still steaming from his nostrils, two cows stamping their feet behind him.

Up in the pole barn, exhausted, limp, waiting, were the sheep and lambs. She could hear and smell them, but could hardly see them. More snow had fallen off the roof, surrounding them in impassable drifts and mounds of ice. The flock was too weak and tired to move, and too frightened. Rose heard Winston crowing in the barn, perhaps calling to one of his hens, who had wandered out into the storm and disappeared.

Looking up through the snow and the mist, Rose stopped.

She saw the line of dark shapes barely visible against snow-banks behind them. They were coyotes, no longer bothering to hide. They were gathering.

And they were watching her. There were no machines to fear, no humans, not even a second dog. The coyotes drifted in and out of sight, as the snow thickened and waned, and that made them seem even more ghostly. It appeared to Rose that they were on the move even though they were sitting still, waiting and watching.

Her mind was quiet, the images gray, almost moribund. She had never been so tired, so weak, or so confused. She had been jolted just a day earlier by her choices, but now there were none left.

She made her way past the barn. Inside, Winston and the hens were prowling the barn floor, pecking for bits of grain. Of all the animals on the farm, they were perhaps best suited to survive such a storm. They could eat almost anything, and they were so thin-blooded they could handle extreme cold as long as they had some semblance of shelter.

She looked through the hole in the back of the barn. Brownie was still standing, although he looked weak and was barely moving. He might not survive too many more days of such cold and wind, so little food.

There was nothing for Rose to do in there. She had a sense of her own limits—of having reached them.

Then, one idea emerged from the others. Two more ewes were lying in the snow, weakened during the march back up the hill. A shivering lamb lay between them. Rose knew it was the lamb she and Sam had pulled out of the ewe that night that seemed like such a long time ago now. Rose would not let these sheep freeze to death in the snow.

She made her way slowly up the hill. It was snowing still, and the cold shot up through her paws and into her bones. It was hard to see through the ice and snow crust on her eyes.

She pushed on to the edge of the pole barn. Normally, the sheep would have sprung to their feet, ready to move, up the hill to the pasture, or down to the feeders near the barn. Today, they lay still. Now for the first time in her life, she knew she could not get them up. And she had no reason to try; there was nowhere to take them.

She met the flock's hungry gaze again, and they looked back at her with the same feelings of fatigue and appeal. Had she come to take them to grass? Old instincts die hard.

One or two stirred, but Rose broke off eye contact and calmly surveyed the survivors. The map in her head was being rewritten again, and it was grim, smaller.

Rose went around the pole barn and sat on the other side, facing up the hill, where the coyotes could see her.

There, out in the snow, she would wait.

This was her place, in front of her sheep, guarding the flock, keeping them safe to the end. This was her work, her destiny, the point of her. Katie flashed into her head, her calm, sure voice. Rose, too, felt calm and sure.

To get them to pasture, to give them time to eat, to protect them. To keep them from ravines and gullies into which they could fall, streams in which they could drown, woods in which they could wander and become lost. To get them home before dark. She did this for them, and to serve the humans her kind served, who had worked with her line all the way back through time.

She kept them safe. She would do that now, whether Sam was here or not, whether it was possible or not.

Until this storm, Rose had never lost a ewe or ram, never

lost a sheep to a ravine, a stream, a coyote, had never shown any less than complete vigilance and care.

Had Sam been in the farmhouse and looked out, he would have been amazed to see this solitary dog, covered in a coating of white, staring up the hill, giving eye to the wind, the snow, the coyotes, to life and the world, to her choices and her duty. He would have marveled at her responsibility, her loyalty, and her bravery. Rose had never run, never backed down, never failed to get it done. He had said that about her so many times—he bragged about her like she was his child, although never in her presence. It would have been patronizing, even insulting, to praise Rose too much to her face. Work was her reward.

But there was no one to see this dog on the hill, and no human would ever know what was about to happen there.

Rose closed her eyes as the snow gathered on her fur, and the cold sank deeper into her bones. She dreamt of the sun, of fresh water, of running through the woods, heading off the sheep, loping in the wind. She dreamed of Katie and her stories, and Sam and his work, and the wild dog, sleeping safely in the house, where he could survive the cold. She dreamed of so many dogs, of sheep and goats and cows, over so many years.

For a moment, she closed her eyes.

The wind told her a million stories, and this was her favorite thing, her favorite dream. Running down the path, hearing the woods, and there, at the end of the path, was Katie, waiting for her, waiting to give her some food, to talk to her.

Then she opened her eyes.

She turned up to the gray sky and she howled, a haunting, piercing wail that cut through the storm and bounced off the barns and out into the woods and off the snow-covered trees.

All the animals who heard it paused and listened, and many trembled.

SHE BLINKED AWAKE, shook the snow off.

She tipped her head toward the coyotes at the edge of the woods. It seemed natural that she and they would be at different ends of this hill, in this storm. She had this strange sensation that she had dreamt of this day, experienced it before.

By now the little dog was almost invisible in the snow. She saw a thousand hills and meadows, too many sheep to count, fires and windstorms, lightning and floods, barns and houses, and it seemed that her images went further and further back, that the storm had opened doors inside her head and she was rushing past them in time, almost too fast to see clearly, through so many blue lights, so many spirits.

UP AT THE top of the hill, the coyote saw that his moment had come. The little dog had come out and lay down, opening herself up to him. The sheep were in the den behind her, weak and vulnerable. He saw the bodies of the cows and steers, almost frozen where they stood. The dog was speaking to him. She was saying, this is the time. Neither she nor he had human notions of victory or defeat.

They simply did what they did. And what happened was what happened. It meant nothing more to them.

The coyote saw that two or three of the cows were alive but barely able to move. He would not attack the big brown one. He would let him die and then feast off the remains.

He had seen the other dog go into the house—they would never go into places where humans lived.

So it was his time. He was cautious, and looked carefully around, for other dogs, for humans. He raised his nose to take in any scents, and pricked his ears for strange sounds. He found nothing and was satisfied. He knew there were cats in the barn, and chickens, but coyotes did not go into barns or buildings. That was the work of lesser animals—foxes, raccoons. Coyotes hunted in the open.

He turned to the other coyotes. They all knew the plan, communicated through body language, eyes, turns of the head.

Three of them went off to the left, moving slowly down the hill to flank the dog on one side and cut off any escape for the sheep. Three went off and circled to the right. Both groups would go below Rose and the pole barn, so that the sheep would have nowhere to run when the coyotes closed in from above, the one with the blue eyes and his den.

They would all move in at once, yipping and barking, circling and charging, tearing at throats, killing quickly, spreading panic, feasting there and hauling off meat back to the den, for them and for their pups.

The dog was weak and tired and could not stop the pack, and even if she fought—for he saw that she would fight—she would be killed quickly.

The coyote leader lay and waited until the other coyotes were down the hill and in place.

Rose saw the coyotes beginning to circle. She knew they were ready to attack. She began a low growl, and her ruff went up. She would fight.

Her mind seemed to be running off without her, still racing back through time, to different places, new scenes, powerful and disturbing images. She imagined being more powerful, wished to find some story to draw from, some memory to call upon. She found none.

She sat up, shook off the snow, waited.

Rose felt at ease, a sense of resignation. The snow swirled around her in little tornadoes, the wind howled loudly down the hill. All of the other animals, sensing what was coming, were still. She peered up at the hill. There was no movement.

THE COYOTE LEADER yipped, a chilling chorus echoing back and forth through the wind and dark and the blowing snow. The signal given and received that the hunt was on, the pack was to move in for the kill. He lowered his head, took the lead, and headed straight for the little dog, who stood up to face him.

The wind was blowing into his face, the ice made footing difficult, the snow was thick, and from time to time he could hardly see the form of the dog. He felt no emotion about killing her—it was what had to be done, and he would do it— though he felt the respect the two of them had had, each for the other from the first.

He loped down the hill. He saw the others in place, advancing from the left and the right, deferring to him, expecting him to draw the first blood. The winds whistled and shrieked, ruffling fur, sending up swirls of snow in the darkness.

Rose looked up, into the storm. She could run, or she could fight. To stay still and be taken was not a choice.

The coyote in front of her hesitated, advanced, then slowed to a crawl, perhaps a change in strategy or an effort to distract or confuse her. As he slowed, the two to her right closed in, just as one did from the left.

She was now uncertain where the attack would come from, and she saw that this was deliberate. She couldn't look everywhere at once, especially if the coyotes were using the blinding snow as cover.

She turned to one side and was surprised to feel a powerful, slashing bite in her opposite shoulder, meant for her throat but thrown off because she had moved. She plunged her teeth into the nose of one of the coyotes, who yelped and jumped back. Then two others were upon her, and she felt piercing bites in her legs and, again, in her shoulder. Herding dogs were not fighters; they were runners. They did not have strong jaws or powerful bites. She knew her teeth were no match for coyotes.

She smelled blood, and her head became light as she collapsed on the ground. She saw the stains in the snow, and heard the sheep crying out in alarm, awaiting the coyotes. She heard the labored breathing of the cows, and the heartbeats of lambs, and the frustrated barks of the wild dog. She looked out for Sam and for Katie but did not see them. The coyotes circled her, pressing their leader to make the kill, and she felt the energy draining from her body in blood, in weariness, in uncertainty. No choices now, as the cold seeped into her bones and traveled up toward her heart.

She thought one more time of Sam and Katie, and she thought of her mother, and the sheep, and felt a great failure settle over her. She could no longer protect them.

She felt peace, too, accepting that perhaps her work was finally done, that there would be rest in the land of the blue lights that she had dreamed about.

THE COYOTE LEADER growled a warning to the others to back off. The little dog was injured, bleeding, nearly done. It was his job, his work, to finish the kill.

He would not eat the body of the dog, nor would he permit the other coyotes to do so. She had to be killed, but she would not be prey. He had his own code for how things were done, and she had earned his respect. She was linked to them, though following a different way. In a different time, it could have been him looking up that hill, or her looking down it.

He stood over her body. She was still breathing, though weakening, and the stain of her blood was spreading through the snow. She curled her lip, and then closed her eyes as if to wait. She did not try to run or show any weakness or fear or deference to him. Her eyes flashed open as he lowered his head, and suddenly she lashed out and took a piece out of his lower lip, startling him and causing him to leap away. Her eyes glowed with challenge.

He stepped back, preparing to charge this time, preparing to tear her throat.

As the coyote drew close, the fur on his ruff came up, and a new smell entered his nostrils. He froze. The snow was falling heavily again, and a fierce gust of wind drove ice into his eyes. He turned his head away. The dog was lying on her side, barely breathing, bleeding, too weak to stand up.

He did not move, his hackles straight up, his ears tilted, his eyes wide, his back stiff.

He heard an awful piercing howl, rolling up the hillside, echoing off the stricken barns and farmhouse, so loud and deep and frightening it seemed to bounce off the sky.

It was angry, urgent, ancient, and it would freeze the soul of any animal who heard it.

The coyote had only heard that howl once before. And he knew it, and knew its meaning.

It was the howl of a wolf. And it was so loud it seemed to cut through him and chill his blood.

He looked down at the dog, but she was no longer there.

In her place, where her dying body had just lain, was an

enormous wolf, with yellow eyes, a long tongue hanging out one side, a thick chest and body, a dense ruff heavy with snow. The wolf was huge, and the coyote could not see past him. With one turn of the head, it had picked up one of the coyotes circling Rose, slashed his throat and thrown his carcass onto the snow, a message delivered so easily and gracefully it could almost have been missed.

The wolf had an enormous, powerful jaw, with blood dripping from its teeth. There was no sign of the little dog. The sheep were silent, paralyzed in terror, frozen in place.

Apart from the wind, a deathly silence settled over the farm. Down by the farmhouse, the coyote saw the wild dog—confused, limping—struggling toward them through the snow. But he couldn't make it, dropping to the ground not far from the door.

The wolf seemed to grow in size as he came closer, eyes blazing. The great creature, many times the size of the coyotes, locked his gaze onto the coyote leader. Then he broke off eye contact and raised his head and howled again up at the storm, into the night sky. It was a sound so wrenching, so angry and powerful, it seemed to turn back the wind, blow back the snow, transform the very air, create its own whirlwind, another kind of storm to challenge the blizzard.

It was the oldest sound, one that had power and meaning going back to the farthest reaches of time.

The coyote's fur was up, and he was backing up the hill now. The other coyotes had all vanished, off through the snow, back into the woods.

They would not be back, this or any other night.

The coyote turned, and then he ran, unable to look back at the unbearable sight.

FOURTEEN

THE SKY WAS BLUE, NOT A CLOUD IN SIGHT.

From the window of the National Guard helicopter Sam could see the farm far off in the distance. It was so clear he could see all the way to Vermont.

His right arm was secured tightly by a sling, and his frost-bitten fingers were wrapped in gauze. He was a bit surprised he had won the battle to return to the farm. He had told them his entire livelihood depended on his getting back, and while there was truth to that, he was most tormented by the image of Rose backing away from the helicopter, choosing to remain behind in that awful storm to stay with the farm and the sheep, and the wild dog.

They had relented finally and agreed to carry him back after three days.

He could not imagine that she had survived, but he would never forgive himself if there was any chance she was still alive and he stayed put, coddled in some hospital bed. Peering out the window, he was crushed by the devastation he saw below him—collapsed barns, fallen trees, downed power lines and impassable roads, dead cows, frozen and stiff in their pastures.

The news reports were horrific: five days of snow, subzero temperatures, and raging winds that topped seventy-five miles per hour. One of the older farm couples had been found dead in their farmhouse, and one or two others were missing. The damage was expected to be staggering. How could a farm survive that kind of havoc, and how could a dog, even one as dedicated and smart as Rose?

The Guard officials understood, after hours of pleading, after he threatened to get dressed and hitchhike back, so when the skies cleared and the flying was finally safe, they took him up. He would have to be lowered back down, the same way he came up.

The doctors were worried about his arm, which had been broken in two places. But they would be leaving him with food, a bigger generator, and a portable electric heater, plus officials expected power back within a week or so. Emergency plowing crews were already trying to clear the roads, so he and two other farmers—a husband and wife and their two small children from Bunker Hill Road—were being choppered back to their farms.

When he told the pilot the story of Rose, they agreed to drop him first, along with three or four bales of hay. But although he expected just about anything from the news reports he'd been hearing, he was still shocked by what he saw from the window as the pilot circled the farm twice, looking for the best place to set him down.

He would have hardly recognized the farm were it not for part of the slate roof of the big barn sticking up out of the snow like a ship marooned in ice. The house was buried in drifts nearly all the way up to the second floor. The barn roof had collapsed. He saw one dead cow lying on its side, the others standing stiffly behind the barn. He could see some sheep lying inside the barn, which was completely surrounded by drifts, but from far up above he could not tell if they were alive or dead.

Up behind the pole barn, he saw another animal body and his heart nearly stopped. It took him a moment to make out that it was a coyote. Even from up high, he saw the stains of blood beside it in the snow. Dear God, he thought, what could have killed a coyote? Certainly not Rose.

He wondered where Rose could possibly be, but as soon as the question crossed his mind, his heart sank again; he knew it was impossible she could have survived any kind of a battle with coyotes, tough and determined though she was. Maybe she ran. But, no, she wouldn't. Not Rose. And if she were alive, wouldn't she have run out to investigate the helicopter, to see if he was coming home?

The pilot pointed to the pasture area behind the barn as the only spot the chopper could get low enough to put him down. They would send someone down with Sam to help him get back into the farmhouse through the drifts, to get some hay to the animals. He was desperate to get back on the ground. Barely a minute had gone by that he wasn't beating himself up for leaving in the first place.

The pilot handed him a walkie-talkie and told him to radio if he needed help in the coming days.

Sam wondered what would be left, wondered if he could really survive here now. And he couldn't get the image of Rose, standing alone in the doorway, out of his mind. He looked out the chopper window, unable to imagine that she wouldn't be outside waiting for him.

He steeled himself as one of the Guardsmen helped him into a harness, a maneuver made all the more awkward by the sling around his arm. It was hard to reconcile the calm blue skies with the awful, hellish storm that had ravaged the area.

He was lowered slowly to the ground, along with the Guardsman who would accompany him for an hour or so, until the chopper circled back to pick him up on the way out again. The snow blew up in a cloud, and Sam looked for the spot where he had been buried, where Rose had dug him out. He saw the animals looking over at him from afar, rattled by the helicopter. They were moving, he was relieved to see.

But he didn't see Rose.

She probably would have made a stand against the coyotes, he knew. He might not even be able to get up to the pole barn to see what had happened until some of the snow began to melt.

The Guard said they might be able to get the roads cleared in a day or so, but there were no promises. They were also putting together a plan to drop hay to trapped animals, and they'd given him a number to call. A chopper had been by earlier, in fact, and dropped some bales near the pole barn and out to the cows. Now that they were closer, Sam could see it, and also see the tracks proving that at least some of the animals had gotten to it.

The pilot had made a note of the pole barn and said he would try and get back and drop some more bales from the air, once they had checked all of the farms for human rescue. There were still people trapped inside their homes without heat, he said, and of course they would be his first priority.

"Good luck finding your dog!" one of the Guardsmen shouted as they lowered Sam from the belly of the helicopter. He landed softly in the snow, which came up to his knees, unlatched the harness, and then stood back as the chopper quickly rose again, veering over to the farmhouse to lower some food and the portable heater.

The Guardsman who came down with Sam was young and fit, exuding calm and competence. He spoke quietly and with authority, and also showed real concern. He bristled with equipment—earphones, gauges, flashlights, clips, kits. Clearly, he had done this before.

The chopper would come back for him and leave Sam there if it seemed safe enough. Sam told himself there was no way they were taking him off the farm again, no matter what he found there.

The Guardsman helped tramp a path to the barn door, and together they signaled that it was all right for the helicopter to take off. Sam told the Guardsman that the first thing they had to do was find Rose, and then get that hay out to the animals.

The sliding door was blocked by snow, but a smaller swinging door was built into it, and it opened after Sam banged it free with his left fist and the Guardsman pulled it open.

The two climbed inside. "Rose, Rose!" Sam yelled, "Are you here? Rose?" He knew she surely wasn't, but he couldn't acknowledge that yet.

Sam heard the sheep calling out from the pole barn, excited to hear the sound of his voice, and he was relieved that at least some of them were okay.

But he gasped when he entered the dark and once open workspace of his big barn. The roof had collapsed in the rear, and there was heavy snow piled everywhere. More surprisingly, the rear doors appeared to have been busted open. Two chickens huddled in their nest, one dead. He saw Winston over in a corner, alive but just barely. He showed the Guardsman where the feed can was and they tossed some of it over to Winston, who awoke and pecked hungrily at it.

There were fallen beams, slate tiles, and debris everywhere. Sam saw the dead, trampled ewe by the rear of the barn and could not imagine how she came to be there. When he walked through the snow and out the back of the barn, he saw most of his cows, alive but trembling where they stood, as he had observed from the helicopter. Brownie, he saw, was lying down by the back of the barn, but he was breathing. When he and the Guardsman yelled and stomped their feet, the old steer struggled to his feet.

The Guardsman ran out to the drop zone, grabbed a bale of hay, and threw some down in front of Brownie, then scattered the rest among the other cows. Some of the bales from the earlier drop had already been eaten.

Sam knew that if he could feed Brownie and get him moving, he would save him. The Guard had also dropped a portable generator, and the Guardsman said he would get it up and running to power water for the house as soon as they found the dog.

Sam had tried to push Rose to the back of his mind. What he most dreaded now was finding her body.

What if she was buried in the snow and he didn't find her till spring? Or if he never found her? What if the coyotes had dragged her off?

He might have cried, but not now, not in front of the Guardsman. The young man was saying he could tie a rope to a bale and drag it up to the pole barn for the sheep who had survived. Sam thought he heard a cry or two from some lambs as well as sheep. The hay feeder was completely iced over. How could any of them have survived this, not to mention the cold, which had plummeted to thirty below?

Then he heard a low, rumbling growl. He turned and tried to locate it. It came from the northeast corner of the barn, from a room he used to store tools and batteries and halters. The young soldier heard it, too. Together, they rushed toward it, kicking away the snow and stepping over the body of the frozen hen. Sam noticed fox tracks in the snow, and he was not surprised.

It took them several minutes to get to the far corner of the barn, through the debris and the snow, the overturned buckets and frozen hoses.

The door to the little storeroom had broken open. It was dark, and when the Guardsman, who was ahead of him, pulled out a flashlight, the growl became more distinct, a bit more menacing. He flashed his light around the dark room.

"Hey," yelled the Guardsman to Sam, "I think I found your dog."

Sam rushed up and looked over his shoulder. "That's not Rose," he said, his heart filling again. But he knew the dog; it was the wild dog, the dog once called Flash. He struggled to his feet, stood, and growled at them, showing his teeth, but there was no real menace in it. Sam knew he was trying to protect something.

He had a sudden memory of the dog riding around in McEachron's battered pickup, and wondered at this creature's long and strange journey, which had ultimately brought him here. He remembered the dog's exhaustion after he'd helped dig Sam out of the snow. He had seen the connection between him and the normally standoffish Rose. Sam dropped to one knee, and the poor old dog nearly collapsed on the ground.

Now that he recognized Sam, he wagged his tail, whined, and offered his nose to Sam's hand. Sam thought he looked more like a skeleton than a dog.

The Guardsman's hand rested on the pistol in his holster, but Sam quickly stepped up and told him it was okay, leaning forward as the dog wavered. The old dog let Sam take his head in his hands.

"You're tired and weak, old man, aren't you?" he said softly, reassuringly. "And you're protecting something. I bet you had a hell of a time here. Let's have a look." He leaned forward, and there, behind the old dog, in the glinting light from the Guardsman's torch, he saw her.

Lying on a pile of rotting old hay was Rose. There was matted blood clotted on her neck and shoulder, and on two of her legs. Her paws were shredded and crusted in blood, her eyes closed, her body still. He couldn't tell whether she was breathing or not.

"My dog, my poor girl," said Sam, and he could not help himself, letting out a sob at the sight of his border collie.

The Guardsman pulled off his gloves and told Sam to wait, then ran out to retrieve his medical pack. While there, he got on his walkie-talkie and asked to be patched through to the local veterinary clinic two towns over.

Sam reached over and touched Rose, stroked her head, felt her body, which was warm, not stiff. She wasn't conscious, but she might be alive. "What happened, girl? What happened here? Be okay—*please.*"

The Guardsman returned and began attending to her.

"There's a heartbeat," he confirmed. "She's alive."

He took out two syringes, injected one, a shot of adrenaline, then the other, a painkiller. He said he'd already gotten clearance to take Rose to the clinic in the chopper when it flew back past this way to pick him up. He said she needed to go, and quickly.

"She's lost a lot of blood, and she's very weak," the Guardsman told Sam. "She got some awful deep wounds." The clinic was right on the way back to their base, he said. Rose's heartbeat was weak, but distinct. There might still be time.

The Guardsman made a litter out of feed sacks and gently lifted the dog into it. She opened her eyes at one point, her tail moved a bit when she looked up at Sam. She leaned forward as if to lick his hand, and Sam put out his one good arm to touch her. "Hey, there," he said, softly, not wanting to excite her.

The Guardsman gave her a mild sedative shot to relax her for the chopper ride. She closed her eyes again, and for a moment Sam thought she was gone.

ROSE HEARD ONLY the breathing of the wild dog, and that only now and then.

She felt disconnected from her body. Different images had been floating through her mind—her mother, the farm, Sam, Katie, the sheep, the wild dog—in a constantly moving blur. She couldn't focus on any one. She was swimming in a pool of darkness, deeper and blacker with each passing minute.

She felt the spirit draining from her. She was beyond exhaustion, the intervals of wakefulness growing shorter, weaker. Day and night had fused into a dank, harsh gray.

Dimly, she heard the wild dog bark and growl, and it awakened her, and then she had another dream, only this time it was of Sam's voice, nearby, quiet and soft and gentle. And then she smelled his hand and knew he was there.

Sam had come back.

She tried to find him, to lick his hand, to wag her tail, but could not move. And she thought of the sheep, and listened for them, but could not hear them.

The painkillers were starting to take hold but she felt great pain all over her body, and then felt herself in motion, which brought on a great wave of dizziness, and then calm.

Sam had returned.

And then she slipped into the darkness.

THE TWO MEN moved her gently out the back, and it wasn't long before they heard the whomp of the chopper returning. The pilot lowered a harness, and they hauled Rose up and secured her in it. She was clearly no longer conscious now, and both men watched as she made the same eerie ascent Sam had made. This time, he was the one to watch her go, perhaps for the last time. This time, he was the one left behind, to manage the farm on his own.

"I can't imagine what went on here," said the Guardsman, as curious as Sam.

The Guardsman also said he could fix up the old dog's wounds, which didn't seem life threatening.

They got more hay out to Brownie and the handful of surviving cows, and then brought feed to the remaining chickens. They put up some temporary boarding to keep out foxes and other predators and tossed hay over the fence of the goat pen, where the goats were all alive and calling out loudly for food.

The Guardsman brought them a bucket of water from the pump, which had finally thawed and was now running. He told Sam all three goats seemed shaken but were fine, complaining with belligerent but healthy voices.

It was the Guardsman who noticed Carol's hooves sticking out through the snow. Sam had been looking all over for her and was not surprised to hear that she was dead. The Guardsman said it did not appear that she had been killed by coyotes, and Sam was almost grateful for that.

"Poor old girl," Sam said to the Guardsman. "She had a rough life. I'm glad she had a few good years here. I hope she died easy."

The Guardsman paused uneasily, but he didn't rush Sam along.

"My father would have been horrified to see me feeding a useless donkey," Sam said. "But I was fond of the old girl, and it was my wife, though—Katie—who really loved her. She brought her carrots every morning, and when Carol was sick and had to have medicine and hot poultices on her legs, Katie came out and played Willie Nelson for her on the boom box. She loved that donkey."

He smiled, and looked over at what he could see of the body.

"And the donkey loved Willie Nelson. Just loved him."

Then he walked away.

The two men climbed up to the pasture as far as they could get, though for Sam that wasn't far. He was in dread pain, and he didn't want to take many painkillers, as he wanted to see what had happened on the farm, and help, if possible. The Guardsman wouldn't let him do much. He reached into one of his kits and gave Sam two pain pills. "My dad was a farmer," he said. "We even had a border collie like yours. Look, I know you're hurting, and nobody can tell you to take it easy. But take it easy."

He held out a hand. "By the way, my name is Kevin," he said.

Sam took it with his good arm. "Sam."

Kevin hauled some hay up on a makeshift sled. The mounds of snow were over their heads in some places, and layers of ice and crusted snow testified to the power of the wind and the cold. Sam saw where an avalanche of snow had fallen off the pole barn roof.

Almost all of the sheep were still alive, even a few weak

lambs, some of them new, still trying to nurse off their exhausted and emaciated mothers. For now, Kevin gave vitamin shots to the lambs. Sam had powdered lamb's milk in the farmhouse, which later they planned to bring out in bottles.

Kevin opened the crate where the generator was, dragged it to the barn, poured oil into it, and cranked it up. It chugged and sputtered to life, and the Guardsman hooked it up to the frost-free hydrant, and to a hose in the barn, as many of the water pipes were cracked and broken. He attached two deicers to it as well, and in a few minutes there was water in the troughs. The animals did not rush to the water, but came slowly, almost one by one, to drink.

Sam was still marveling at having found Rose alive, hoping she survived, and there was almost too much for him to take in, especially with a stranger around. He felt strange without Rose, as if the farm had lost part of its soul. He kept looking around for her, and had to remind himself that she had been taken away. The farm seemed especially desolate without her.

About half an hour later, the pilot radioed to say that Rose was in surgery at the veterinary clinic, and that her condition was "extreme." They would do everything they could, but she had lost much blood and suffered from broken bones, bite wounds, and hypothermia.

KEVIN WAS an experienced hunter and tracker, and Sam knew every inch of the farm. Between them, the two men pored over all the ground around the pole barn, as well as the way back to the farmhouse, piecing together what they could of what had happened on the farm during the last day of the blizzard. It wasn't much.

What astonished the Guardsman were some of the tracks he found. "They're enormous—definitely wolf tracks. I can't figure that part."

Sam was skeptical. Few wolves had been seen around Granville for generations, he said, and what would one be doing on the farm in a storm? Wouldn't it have killed Rose and the wild dog?

Kevin was baffled. He was sure they were the tracks of a single large wolf; he had seen them before out west, and there was a dead coyote with enormous teeth marks on its neck and shoulders. The wolf tracks and dog tracks ran alongside one another, suggesting the two had stood together somehow.

Kevin took out his digital camera and got some close-ups of the prints in the snow. He would send them to the state university for analysis, he said, and maybe they would give him a definitive answer.

Beyond that, both men agreed, it appeared as if Rose was injured defending the barn and the animals. They couldn't be sure of much else. There seemed to be evidence of foxes, and of something breaking down the big barn door, perhaps a panic of the steers and cows.

Kevin carried the wild dog from the barn into the farmhouse, and put him down gently. The old dog put up no resistance. Sam brought him food and water. The Guardsman sedated him, cleaned and dressed his wounds, and gave Sam some antibiotics that were meant for humans, but which would also work on the dog.

"I think he'll make it," said the Guardsman.

"Yeah," said Sam. "He's been through a lot. But he has a home here now—if he'll stay." That was the least he could do for Rose, he thought.

"He'll stay," said Kevin. "He's had enough."

* * *

THE GUARDSMAN couldn't stop talking about the wolf. The odd thing, he said, is that there were no wolf marks on any sheep, or on Rose or the wild dog, only on the coyote, which had been slaughtered quickly, a clean kill. And then the wolf seems to have left.

How could that have happened?

"He was up by the pole barn . . ." he said, almost to himself. "Why wouldn't he have taken one of the sheep? Maybe he dragged one off?"

But he could find no tracks away from the spot where the coyote lay, no tracks leading in or out of the pasture. It was almost, he said, as if he came out of the sky, and left the same way.

Sam said nothing. He would need time to try to sort this out.

Kevin dug out a space around the back door, helped Sam settle into the farmhouse, and cranked up the other emergency generator they had dropped for heat, then radioed that he was ready for the helicopter to come pick him up.

When the chopper arrived, Kevin said he wished the best for Rose, and promised to come back and visit when he could. "You can call the vet and figure out how to bring her back. She'll be there a bit, I guess, and the roads will be better by · then. Good luck, sir. Take it easy, okay?"

He shook Sam's good hand.

"Thank you," Sam shouted over the noise of the rotor. The Guardsman was pulled up into the chopper, and it roared away.

Sam felt a wave of loneliness—for Katie, for Rose, for the farm as it was. He felt the strange absence of Rose, always there with him, always ready. He wondered if she would be coming back.

He was also glad, in a curious way, to be alone, except for the company of the old dog. He didn't know what to make of what he and Kevin had found. He couldn't put it together. He wasn't old, or as set in his ways as his father. He was willing to change, to try new things, but he was still a farmer, and there was nothing in his life or experience to help him understand what might have happened.

He had always believed that dogs were dogs, and should not be seen as anything more, but now he didn't know what to think. It seemed to him as if Rose had somehow saved most of the animals, saved the farm, and that was an idea that was simply beyond him.

He'd already heard about most of the other farms, barns wrecked, almost all of the livestock dead. That was what he expected to find here, what he had prepared himself for.

Sam returned to the house and sat down in the living room. The generator hummed outside the kitchen door, and he was glad to be back at his farm, as awful as all the damage was. He had some insurance, and the government had already promised to help the farmers knocked out by the storm, although he knew that politicians loved to make promises, and government help could be more trouble than the storm itself.

He was almost afraid to think about it. He looked down at the sleeping old dog, and felt a surge of affection for him. He was glad to have him nearby. He'd been a part of whatever had happened.

Sam prayed Rose would survive, but he didn't dare get his hopes up. He would have trouble forgiving himself for leaving her there to face coyotes, and maybe even a wolf.

Sam was exhausted and in pain. The whole year had been

draining, and he was still reeling—from the loss of Katie, the farm's troubles, the grinding responsibilities of running it alone, and now this disaster. What else could happen? But he shook off his self-pity, like his father had always told him to do. Shake off feeling sorry for yourself, like a dog that just came in from the rain.

The sun streamed into the farmhouse through the big living room windows, stronger than ever thanks to the vast reflective whiteness of all that snow. The house itself, he saw, was intact, okay. There was no major damage inside. He was, for a moment, hopeful. He might get his life back, or at least some of it. He might even get his dog back. He prayed it was so, thinking of Rose undergoing surgery, wishing her strength and safe passage, steeling himself for the worst. He wished he had someone to talk to about it, but he didn't. And most likely wouldn't.

He looked down again at this equally exhausted old dog and again was surprised at the affinity he felt for him. He hadn't wanted another dog, had always resisted the idea.

"Hey," he said. "You have a home here if you want one."

Flash stirred, clambered to his feet, his tail wagging, and ambled over to look at Sam. He put his forelegs on the sofa beside him, too weak to pull himself up all the way.

"I bet it's been a long time since you slept on something soft," Sam said, as much to himself as the dog.

With his good left arm, Sam leaned over and pulled him up. The dog sighed deeply, and sank into sleep. He spent the night with his head in Sam's lap.

Sam, however, kept tossing and turning, expecting Rose to come in and check on him. But she wasn't there.

FIFTEEN

A WEEK AND A HALF AFTER ROSE WAS LIFTED OUT, SAM GOT A call from the vet saying Rose could come home. But the vet was adamant: Even if she had to be tied up or crated, Rose had to rest. And not just for days, but months. She needed quiet. She had undergone extensive surgery, blood transfusions, stitching, and bone repair. She had pins in one leg.

She had to be walked on a leash and given her pills—painkillers and antibiotics. No running, no working. Sam smiled when he heard that. Rose had never been on a leash in her life. And had never rested either that he could remember.

Like most farmers, Sam was wary of vets, and paid little attention to their recommendations. What did they know, except how to mail out bills?

But he reassured the vet—yes, he would be careful. He was too excited about getting his dog home to worry about the rest of it. After Rose was airlifted to the hospital, things had been up and down with her for several days. The doctor had been so guarded on the phone that Sam had been preparing himself for the worst.

When the day finally came, the vet said he was heading out to tend to some cows on a nearby farm and he would drop Rose off on his way.

It was a crisp, clear day. The signs of the storm were still everywhere—mounds of snow and ice, crushed barns and out-buildings, potholes in roads, fallen trees and downed wires, holes in roofs, drainpipes and gutters hanging askew, twisted gates and bowed fences.

But the skies could not have been calmer or prettier, and it even felt a bit mild. Standing on the porch, Sam listened to the drip of melting snow everywhere, contrasting this day with the awful days of the blizzard. "Nature can really swing both ways, can't it, dog?" he observed to Flash. The old dog looked up at him, tail wagging.

WHEN THE GREEN SUV pulled up, Sam was standing by the road, sipping from a mug of coffee, where he had been ever since the vet phoned to say he was on his way. Flash was still sitting next to him, both of them watching the road. "We could be a postcard," Sam had joked to Flash, who wagged his tail in response to Sam's tone, lighter than it had been.

Flash growled when the big SUV pulled into the drive-way, then quieted. The farm was his territory now, and he was inclined to be possessive of it, especially in Rose's absence.

The vet, a tall, thin man with sandy brown hair, turned off the ignition, got out, shaking Sam's hand as he glanced down at Flash. "He's looking good, Sam," he said. "You've done a great job with him."

Sam was pleased to hear that. He had cleaned the old dog's wounds, changed his bandages every day—the Guardsman and some neighbors had come by to help and brought medicine and vitamins, gotten him moving, massaged his sore old joints. He *had* done a good job. But that didn't matter now. He needed to see Rose.

When he came around to the back of the SUV and looked inside, he saw that Rose was in a crate, lying still. She lifted her head and looked up at him, her tail moving softly back and forth. Even then, he could see what a mess she was, what she had been through. He took a sharp, deep breath. Happy as he was to see her, it was a shocking sight.

Ever the beautiful, athletic dog, she was a quilt of patches, bare skin, bruises, wounds, and stitches. She looked drawn, and her forelegs and ribs were swathed in bandages, some from surgical wounds, others from IV tubes, still more from injuries. Her shoulder was wrapped in heavy gauze; her right leg was in a soft cast, which stuck out strangely behind her.

Sam looked up at the vet.

"I know it seems bad, but it looks worse than it is at this point," he said. "We were lucky to save her, and she'll need time to recover. But she'll be all right, Sam. She won't have a hundred percent mobility, but she'll still be faster than most dogs. She wouldn't eat much at the hospital. Try to get some food into her, will you? And she has a bunch of pills. Make sure she takes them. All labeled. She's a stoic dog, strong. We put her through a lot, and she never complained or gave us any trouble. Unless we tried to pet her. Make sure she doesn't move much."

Rose kept looking at her leg, which seemed to be separate from her body, and at the cast, which she clearly intended to remove as soon as she could. In fact, the vet told Sam, she had removed it several times already. He said he wouldn't even try to put a cone on her.

Sam looked at the vet and nodded, a surge of affection rising in his chest. He always found it amusing when vets told him to keep Rose still. He doubted any of them had ever had a border collie like her.

Rose struggled to stand up, and slowly, with small steps, moved to the back of the crate. Sam was afraid to move her, afraid to hurt her, she looked so frail. He looked at the vet, who put one arm gingerly under Rose's stomach, the other on her collar, and gently lifted her down to the ground. Then he took out a leash and clipped it onto Rose's collar. "That's how to pick her up if you have to. I don't want her jumping." Sam took the leash from him, holding it a bit awkwardly.

"Listen, Sam, no working. I mean it. I can't even guess at what she must've gone through to have wounds like that— never seen it before. A hard run could open her up, even kill her."

Sam said he understood. He closed his hand around the leash and looked down at his dog. "Okay, Rose, welcome home."

Rose stepped forward gingerly, her leg dragging awkwardly. Her tail was going back and forth slowly, and her head was lowered, almost as if she were shy. She came to Sam, sniffed, then nuzzled his hand, and licked it once. Flash approached her, and the two of them touched noses, their tails going faster now as the older dog sniffed her bandages and wounds.

Sam knelt down on the ground. He trembled a bit as he pressed his head gently against hers. Several tears rolled down the sides of his face.

Rose accepted the hug, returning it with soft licks.

Sam shook hands with the vet, thanked him, and as the SUV pulled off, he slowly led Rose toward the back of the farmhouse.

There, Sam took the leash off. "I've never put a leash on you, girl, and I'll trust you to stay put right here and take it easy, okay?"

ROSE, WALKING SLOWLY, understood. There was no work in Sam's tone. With the wild dog behind her, she walked on the path cleared through the snow.

She lifted her nose, looked at the hillside, saw the tracks, her instincts and senses collecting the story of the storm, telling it back to her, remembering it, storing it away. For a long time, she stared at the hill, raising her nose high into the air. Sam watched her.

The winterscape was still striking, imposing mounds of snow everywhere, wood and slate all over the ground. Still, it was very different from the last time she had seen it.

Rose saw the Blackface and the sheep gathered in front of the pole barn. She looked over to where she had seen Carol die, gazed into her sad eyes, said her good-bye.

She narrowed her eyes at the spot where she had faced the coyotes.

Several of the sheep called out to her, and she returned their gaze. None of them moved. She realized that she looked strange to them, that some of them didn't recognize her—it had been nearly two weeks, and she was covered in bandages.

The Blackface did know her, though, and held her gaze, a gesture of respect, it seemed to Rose, an acknowledgment of some kind.

She looked up the hill, where she had gone to collect the goats, and to the upper pasture, where she had lain when she'd seen the place of blue lights and the spirit of her mother.

Up on her left, the goats began jeering and complaining

and calling out to her, making little sense. They seemed to feel that Rose had authority on the farm, and so they made demands on her. They wanted more food, as usual. She ignored them, as usual.

She limped a few steps to her right, and through the fence she could see Brownie and the cows grazing at the feeder. They did not look at her. She heard Winston crowing in the barn, and heard his hens clucking. He sounded as if he were back to his old self, officious, even pompous.

Rose saw damage everywhere. Her map had changed; everywhere she looked, her landscape and bearings were rearranged. There was a lot to take in.

Slate had fallen off the farmhouse roof, there were gaping holes in the roof of the barn, and several of the gates were off their hinges. Much of the glass in the barn windows was broken, the panes blown out. The wind had knocked trees and poles down.

She closed her eyes and could hear, far behind her, the sounds of hawks soaring above, seeking food, the animals in the woods out foraging, hunting, digging. She listened for any sound from the coyote, but heard none. She could smell the animals and leaves and brush emerging from the snow, and hear the lowing of cows from farms miles away.

She was orienting herself, after lost days, fuzzy images, time in crates. She listened for Katie, raised her nose, hoping to pick up her scent. But she didn't hear her or smell her.

Sam was silent, watching Rose's homecoming, giving it space and respect. The wild dog was sitting down, quiet and observant. He could stop searching for her now.

Rose looked up into Sam's eyes—for a moment—and then around at the farm again. She turned, walked toward the pasture on paths and trails that had been cleared.

Sam raised his hand, as if to caution her, but when she turned and glanced at him, he lowered his arm. She made her way slowly to the pasture gate, hauling her cast, shaking her head to brush off the pain. She managed to slowly crawl under it, moving up toward the pole barn, where the sheep collected themselves into a flock and lowered their heads to study her.

She sat.

She considered her map, and, almost unconsciously, changed it. She removed a cow, a dead lamb, the donkey, a ewe, and a hen.

She kept Katie in her map, and scanned the farm once again for her, reflexively. She was not in the pasture, or out in the woods. And she was still not, Rose could sense, in the farmhouse. She looked back at the wild dog, who was sitting beside Sam, watching her.

Her vision was blurred at times, and her body ached. She felt a strange stiffness in her side from the wounds, the bandages, the broken ribs and aching bones. Simply breathing was painful, slow. She knew not to run or jump. And for once, she knew not to work, not yet.

Rose looked around again, at the sheep, at Sam.

Finally it seemed she had seen what she needed to see, knew what she needed to know. She closed her eyes, raised her nose high into the air.

Slowly, almost laboriously, she lay down in the pole barn near the sheep, who stirred nervously. She closed her eyes and tried to dream her dream, her favorite one, of the sheep crunching away in the meadow on grass rippling in the wind, shining in the sun.

EPILOGUE

BY SUMMER, THE FARM WAS ITS LUSH, SMELLY, VERDANT self—recognizable, Sam thought, if not quite the same as last year. The corn and alfalfa were high and green, the barns had purplish new slate roofs. The outer pasture was full of cows and more than a score of lambs darted playfully in and out of the pole barn. Blackflies and mosquitoes swarmed everywhere.

The community had banded together, as farm communities do, to help get all of the farms up and running. There were still signs of damage on most houses and barns, but the storm already seemed remote to many, another drama of life in a long series. Farmers knew dramas. Sam had seen many.

Death and trouble are routine, an integral part of farm life. There are always chores, crops, work to pull you along.

Some neighbors had come by to help Sam repair his fences and gates, many of which were damaged in the crush of snow and ice. They fixed tarpaulins over the holes in the barn, and rebuilt the big barn doors.

The reports of the wolf had spread quickly through the

county, causing something of a panic. Farmers got out their shotguns and rifles, and county and state wildlife agents prowled the woods looking for tracks. But no wolf had been found, no tracks discovered. It was rarely mentioned much anymore, although Sam still took his rifle when he went out at night. He had seen the dead coyote up by the barn.

Rose remembered that night, too. Sam noticed that Rose behaved strangely up near the pole barn, where she often paused, sniffed the ground, her ruff rising up.

JUST AFTER DAWN, Rose was in the habit of going into the pantry, where the wild dog slept near the woodstove, and sniffing him awake. He was slow to rouse and would stretch his stiff legs and forepaws, then stand and lap up some water. Then he and Rose would slip out the dog door before Sam was ready to head out and do chores. Since the storm, Sam now spent some time in the mornings on the computer, always muttering about red tape, forms, and regulations for claiming insurance and grants.

Rose had no idea what he was doing, or why, but had adapted to the new, slightly later schedule. This was when she and the wild dog went for their walk around the farmhouse and in the fields nearby.

SAM NOTICED that since the storm, Rose spent more time by herself than she had before, out in the barn, or on the path. She was often with Flash, who was too frail to chase after sheep but who loved to sit with her in the barn or watch her from the pasture gate while she worked. The two often spent the evenings together, either by the woodstove, where the heat made her leg more comfortable, or in Katie's old sewing room.

Flash took pills for worms and parasites, for arthritis and heart disease, and for his aching joints. But he had recovered amazingly well from his previous wretched condition and settled happily into life on a farm again, even if he couldn't work.

Flash loved sleeping in the dark and musty corners of old barns, and stayed close to the woodstove on cold nights. He had taken over the old black sofa, which he sometimes deigned to share with Sam. He loved the morning and evening servings of kibble, and he sensed that Sam had formed a strong attachment to him.

SAM SENSED IT too. If Rose was Sam's working dog, then Flash became something of a pet. Rose hated to leave the farm, and sometimes got sick in trucks—upset by the motion, to which she was especially sensitive. In Flash, Sam had a companion for the endless riding around that came with country life. Sam could see that Flash enjoyed this, and it became his new work. Sam took Flash everywhere he went, and Rose would often look up as the truck rolled off down the hill, Flash's head sticking out the window, taking in the smells and sights of the dens, caves, and woods where he had lived for so long.

AS FOR ROSE, she sensed that the wild dog's company made Sam happier, more cheerful. This was work that she could not do. Rose sometimes felt possessive or territorial, but envy was not known to her. She understood the wild dog's need to work, and Sam's need for him.

One morning, a crisp, early summer day with mist coming up in the pasture and over the hills beyond, Rose came into the pantry and Flash was not there. She knew he wasn't in the house—she couldn't smell or hear him.

She did hear the sheep calling out, though not in alarm. They seemed confused, the way they were when something was out of the ordinary. It could mean the appearance of a groundhog, a fox, an airplane, a skunk.

She went out through the swinging dog door into the cool sunny morning, so different from the snow and ice of the big storm. Rose looked up toward the pole barn, where the sheep were, and paused. After a moment, she started running, streaking across the rear of the farm to the pasture gate, slipping under it and up alongside the big barn, gathering speed as she went, pumping up the hill. She didn't see him until she got closer, although she already knew he was there.

Up by the side of the pole barn, lying on his side, was Flash.

From some distance away, Rose could hear the wheeze in his breath, his faint heartbeat. He was laboring badly, his tongue hanging from one side of his mouth. He must have gotten up sometime during the night, crept out the door, and come up into the pasture. He would not have chosen to die inside a house.

Instead he chose to die with the sheep, as any farm dog might.

When she reached him, Rose sniffed his tail, then his side, then touched his nose. She could hear the weak pumping of blood in his veins, the labored breathing, the rattle in his throat.

She had known, of course, well before she reached him.

It was not a bad feeling. She saw an image of the emaciated

old dog seeking sanctuary as the blizzard approached. He was different now.

She had seen the wild dog settle in happily at the farm, attaching himself to Sam in a way she never could, curling up each night on his fluffy dog bed, living his last days in comfort and surrounded by affection. She saw how content he had been.

She knew he was blind in one eye, nearly deaf, and lame in two legs, and that his knees and joints were sore and swollen. She smelled the blood connection, and felt it, too; the two had been joined in the most powerful way ever since the storm.

All of the animals on the farm gazed up, some uneasily, at the odd sight of the two dogs together beside the pole barn, one smelling so distinctly of death.

A few flies already buzzed around Flash, and Rose looked up to see vultures circling high in the air. There were scavengers on the ground, too, out of sight—foxes, coyotes, and birds and raccoons. Once his spirit left, Rose had no interest in his decaying body. The scavengers could have him.

She sat down next to her father, who opened his eyes, and whose breath was a throaty wheeze. His eyes were glazed, out of focus, and his hind legs were splayed, one of them twitching in spasm.

The sheep were now watching, anxious. An impulse to go get Sam flashed through her mind, but she looked at Flash and she felt *his* instincts: He wanted to be alone, with her, with the sheep, in the pasture.

It was over for him. Rose felt no grief, just a responsibility to be with him on this passage.

ROSE DID NOT LEAVE Flash's side that morning.

Up on this hill, the sun burning off the mist, the two dogs

fused in their own particular fantasy. The other animals turned away. It was alien to them, unsettling, this scene. The old dog needed to be touched, known, and Rose lay down next to him, and put her nose against his.

This was a crossing for each of them.

The old dog was leaving, and Rose would be living a different kind of life without him. If she did not exactly know grief, she did know loss.

For Flash, this was a journey into the unknown. Rose knew how far she could take him, because she had been there once before. She closed her eyes, and he closed his, and they both entered another space, one quieter than any the wild dog had known, just as Rose had experienced it during the storm.

It was a place of absolute stillness and peace.

They crossed a smooth expanse of water, still and shimmering. They crossed to another shore. Again, there were the blue lights as far as both could see, the countless lights on the far side of the stream.

They both saw they were with the spirits of dogs.

Rose saw the old dog find this place of ease and quiet. She was not there, she was only guiding him. He walked alongside her, slowly, and at first with some pain. But soon that seemed to ease, and his gait smoothed out and his pace quickened, and before long, when they came to the point she could not go past, he simply glided on ahead of her.

He turned to her, their eyes met, and then he turned away and did not look back.

And then she lost him, gone in the seas of blue lights, colors, and the mist into which he seemed to melt.

And just like that, he was gone.

Rose opened her eyes and looked out at the pasture, and

felt the wind. She raised her nose in the air, catching the stories the wind brought, and knew all she needed to know.

She saw that the old dog's eyes were open, but he had stopped breathing; his spirit had whirled up into the sky. She sniffed his snout, and then his forehead, and then sat back up and looked out over the sheep, and the farm.

The sheep called softly to one another, and looked away.

And she heard a door slam down below. Rose saw Sam coming up the hill, a shovel in one hand. She'd heard him earlier calling for Flash, seen him looking out the window. He too must have known what the dog was doing up in the pasture, why he had gone there. Sam had left them alone until he saw the birds circling overhead.

And she saw now that he was looking down at the ground, his face oddly contorted.

She came slowly down to meet him, to walk with him back up the hill.

It was all she could do.

It was enough.

THE FARM was well into the dog days.

Sam had decided to breed Rose, and she was pregnant. The sire was a purebred border collie from Manchester, Vermont. She was calm and ripe, as Sam liked to put it, and he was like a proud and expectant dad.

Rose's pups, he told his friends, had to be special dogs. Other farmers should have them, and Sam wasn't shy about thinking about the money they might bring. The vet said $2,000 a pup would not be unreasonable, perhaps even more, given Rose's spreading reputation. For Sam, for any farmer, that was serious money. Her work in the storm had already become local legend, and some people had even driven by the farm to get a look at her. Sam usually shooed them off.

Sam meant to keep one of the males for himself. To help out on the farm, to ride with him into town. He missed Flash more than he would have imagined or admitted to anyone.

Rose was, in fact, different, although Sam could not say precisely how. Sam thought she seemed somehow calmer, more contemplative, if you could use such a word to describe a dog.

Something about her seemed more settled, almost peaceful, apart from her limp, a reminder of those awful days in the storm. Otherwise, you wouldn't know, Sam thought.

As THE SUMMER PROGRESSED, Rose's belly began to swell. With each day that passed she was growing quieter and rounder. She lazed in the hot days of summer in a way she never had before.

One afternoon, when Sam had gone off in the truck and the farm shimmered in the hazy sun, the animals settled and quiet, Rose felt something stir inside of her. Slowly she made her way down the hill, away from the sheep onto the path, and out to Katie's stump.

She took her time, pausing to smell rabbit holes and scat and listen to mice and chipmunks and bees. She felt a sense of great expectancy.

Rose loved these walks through the woods, the mishmash of smells and sounds and colors that awakened her, and sharpened her senses. The stories of her world were dancing in her head. She could hardly keep up with them, and she felt like spinning for joy.

She felt strong, alive.

And she felt, for the first time in her consciousness, light and free.

And not alone.

When she got to the stump, she lay down.

There was a long pause, and Rose imagined Katie. The two listened to the sound of the creek rushing through the forest, the leaves rustling in the breeze, the birds in the trees, the animals running along the ground and in burrows. They smelled flowers and took in the news of the wind, the changing shadows.

Tell me, Katie asked, was there really a wolf?

Rose glanced up into Katie's eyes, and the two looked into each other's souls. Rose did not understand the words, but tilted her head to try to catch the tone, and picked up the wonder, the admiration, the love.

ACKNOWLEDGMENTS

I thank Jennifer Hershey for her extraordinary hard work and vision in shaping this challenging book and assisting my return to fiction. And Jen Smith.

I also thank Bruce Tracy, Andy Barzvi, Richard Abate, Emma Span, Jane Richter, Brian McLendon, Courtney Moran, Elizabeth Stein, and Maria Wulf.

I appreciate my wonderful dogs—Rose, Izzy, Lenore, and Frieda—who inspire my work and my photography every day.

ABOUT THE AUTHOR

JON KATZ has written nineteen books—seven novels and twelve works of nonfiction—including *Soul of a Dog, Izzy & Lenore, Dog Days, A Good Dog,* and *The Dogs of Bedlam Farm.* He has written for *The New York Times, The Wall Street Journal,* Slate, *Rolling Stone, Wired,* and the *AKC Gazette.* He has worked for CBS News, *The Boston Globe, The Washington Post,* and *The Philadelphia Inquirer.* Katz is also a photographer, and the author of a children's book, *Meet the Dogs of Bedlam Farm.* He lives on Bedlam Farm in upstate New York with the artist Maria Wulf; his dogs, Rose, Izzy, Lenore, and Frieda; his donkeys, Lulu and Fanny; and his barn cats, Mother and Minnie.

www.bedlamfarm.com

ABOUT THE TYPE

This book was set in Granjon, a modern recutting of a typeface produced under the direction of George W. Jones, who based Granjon's design upon the letter forms of Claude Garamond (1480–1561). The name was given to the typeface as a tribute to the typographic designer Robert Granjon.